DEATH
OF A
DEAD MAN

GEORGE MURRAY

GEORGE MURRAY
PUBLICATIONS

DEATH OF A DEAD MAN
(Closing a Cold Case)

Is the intellectual property of the author
GEORGE MURRAY
All rights reserved 2013 © George Murray

Cover design, typesetting and logo design by
PAULA HÖRLING-MOSES
www.macmoses.net

Cover photos by
www.shutterstock.com

Printed in the United Kingdom by
LIGHTNING SOURCE UK LTD
Milton Keynes

Published by
GEORGE MURRAY PUBLICATIONS
Edinburgh
July 2016

ISBN 978-0-9927385-8-7

DEATH OF A DEAD MAN

GEORGE MURRAY

ONE

The search for Laura Purdie had been carried out over several days with volunteers from the local community on the south side of Glasgow repeatedly offering to spend their day, or the available part of it, scouring waste land, demolished buildings, deserted brown field sites and redundant railway lines. The police attempted to co-ordinate their efforts but deployment was difficult and random.

The CID had concentrated their enquiries among the fairground community as the girl had told her mother that she was going to 'the shows' with a friend. Her mother had wondered at her daughter's failure to return home that evening but did not report the girl missing until the following day after contacting the young friend. The two girls had been together at the fairground but had become separated and had not met up again.

A week later, on 28th September 1963, Laura Purdie's body was discovered in woods bordering a public park. She was lying face down and partially clothed on a carpet of brown leaves. The post-mortem examination would determine that she had been raped prior to death by manual strangulation. She was only 15 years of age.

The subsequent police enquiry had led to the arrest and trial, the following year, of a 23 year old man from Glasgow on charges of rape and murder. He had been seen walking with the missing girl among the crowd at the fairground after she had split from her friend. Fragments of brown leaves had been found in the turn-ups of his trousers and inside his shoes.

To the police officers interviewing him at the police station and later to the jurors at the High Court, he had neither admitted nor denied his responsibility for the crimes libelled. He had denied ownership of a brass petrol fuelled lighter found near the body. The lighter was engraved with the initials G.P.

The jury returned a verdict of guilty on the charge of rape and on the murder charge had opted for the lesser charge of culpable homicide after hearing from a forensic surgeon that strangulation could have been committed during the act of rape as a means of control and coercion. A sentence of 18 years imprisonment was imposed by the judge.

Two weeks later, in a cell of Barlinnie Prison, Glasgow, young George Prentice lay flat on his shallow mattress and stared at the ceiling wondering how his life could have gone so horribly wrong.

He had been content in his own solitary way, working each day on the heating systems of large municipal buildings with nobody to bother him except the occasional visit of a boss or some interested but uncritical official of the council department. On his days off he had taken to fishing the canal or walking on the Campsie Hills to the north of the city. Following the death of his mother he had become the sole tenant of the council house he called home. He had come and gone as he wished without bothering anyone. For a man not yet twenty-four, he had retreated ridiculously early from most forms of social behaviour compared to Glasgow men of similar age.

Life had been so different just a few years earlier. He had been so different. Working through his plumbing apprenticeship during the day and training for football in the evenings, George Prentice had developed a large social circle. He had once played on trial with Partick Thistle, a top senior club at the time. On Friday and Saturday nights there were dance halls open late and he had all the confidence required to meet young attractive women.

He remembered as he always did, one girl in particular. Her name was Laura, a name that would haunt him. It haunted him now. In the young life of George Prentice she had been the cherry on the cake, the fairy on the Christmas tree. When she had told him that she was pregnant he had been only a little deflated. His mother would moan but he was not discouraged. Surely this pregnancy would ensure that they remained together. With a baby to care for he and Laura were assured of a future together. They could push on with life, consolidating everything they already meant to each other.

Laura had thought otherwise and had told him so. Child or no child there would be no future together. Laura Turnbull had considered herself as being much too young to be held down in a marriage and as for the pregnancy, she would deal with that in her own way. He wondered if she was repeating the words of her parents. The Turnbulls had then moved away and George Prentice had never seen his Laura since.

His levels of confidence and self-esteem had dropped markedly but he had refused to blame her. He chose to blame himself and had determined never to place himself in such a vulnerable situation again. For the best part of two years he had hoped that he could find Laura and see their child. Had it been a boy or a girl?

She had laughed at him, that young girl at the fairground.

He had been staring at the machinery of the 'Waltzer' when he heard her laughter. It had reminded him of his Laura, the way she once laughed. The girl was right beside him on the boardwalk, leaning against the outside rail. He knew that she was only a teenager but she had been trying to appear older. She had cigarettes and had given him one. He had been too taken aback to say 'no' and he had taken it. She had lit it for him just before lighting her own. He had noticed the lighter she was using and asked to look at it. It was one of these brass lighters, petrol fuelled, very popular at the time. It had the initials 'G.P.' engraved on the front. He had asked her if they were her initials and she had laughed again, 'No stupid, my name is Laura'.

She had taken the lighter back, almost snatching it from him as her streetwise instinct told her that he wanted it. He had offered her two pounds for the lighter, explaining that 'G.P' were his initials. She had refused. She could not sell the lighter because it belonged to someone close to her. He had asked if she meant a boyfriend. She had laughed again but never confirmed his suggestion.

He had walked with her around the fairground, like the witnesses had said in court. He had told her about his own Laura of two years earlier and she seemed sorry for him. She seemed to him to be like his own Laura, back in the early days. He had liked her and she must have liked him to have given him a cigarette and smiled so much. He had bought her a pink candyfloss.

Prentice moved to turn onto his side and the sudden pain brought him out of his reverie. The reason for his solitary confinement had been the attack made on him by his fellow prisoners soon after his admission to the prison. The girl's murder had been headline news for months and the hard men of Barlinnie felt the same about her rape and murder as most other citizens. Prentice had been beaten and kicked unconscious by the time an adequate number of prison officers had intervened. In the interests of his further safety, Prentice had been transferred to a cell on his own. He could expect to remain there for some time until time allowed the anger of others to mellow or at least divert to some new incomer. The solitude did not bother Prentice. If his cell had contained a heating boiler and a tool bag, he could have been quite content for life would be almost back to normal. Life was not normal though and Prentice was far from content.

He was losing his council house, the solicitor had told him that. His older sister had agreed to take what possessions she could reasonably hold for him but most of his belongings would be thrown out. She was helping he supposed, but she seemed to be in no doubt as to his guilt, his own sister. She was wrong, damn it, they were all wrong and one day he would show them. He would put matters right.

Gordon Macrae was twenty-five years older than George Prentice and could not have imagined what it was like to be confined in one small room day after day. His younger years had been spent a long way from Glasgow or any other city. Gordon had been born and raised on a croft in Sutherland, a rugged county in the north of Scotland.

As a child he had walked a distance of three miles, often barefooted, to and from a small primary school. On his return home each day he had simply joined the daily work routine of his crofting family. Both his parents had been fit and active at that time and his older sister would join her mother in the home knitting group of ladies who brought extra income for themselves while enjoying the company. For his father and other crofters life was hard. Their husbandry skills with animals had to be complemented by some capability in carpentry and building maintenance for they could not afford outside labour. The working week consisted of six long days of toil followed by one strictly observed Sabbath day. The Sunday respect was necessary to their faith and the continuing fraternity with neighbours.

Religious congregation, schooling, farming events and the occasional village dance brought the community together. The more personal 'ceilidhs' where families visited one another in their homes had sealed friendships to last a lifetime. All this behaviour had also formed the education of a developing young man. Gordon Macrae had noticed how the local people were not entirely alike. Some had skills in music or singing or story-telling and the presence of such people was always welcome at any ceilidh, almost as welcome as the drams of whisky.

With the outbreak of war in 1939. Gordon Macrae had been summoned from the croft to serve his country as a soldier with the Argyll and Sutherland Highlanders. He had gone ashore at Normandy with the Second Battalion and had fought his way to the banks of the Elbe by the time the war ended.

On his return to Scotland he had resisted the invitations of surviving comrades to remain in the central belt, preferring instead to return to the croft in Sutherland. His parents looked to him to be so much older. Times were no easier and his own contribution was more needed than ever.

Only in 1965, with both his parents dead, did Gordon consider his presence on the croft to be less essential. The only asset on the croft was himself and no-one would blame him now for leaving. He locked the door and walked away, imagining that the landowner would simply take it back in Gordon's absence.

Major construction projects were under way around Glasgow and Gordon Macrae easily gained employment as a labourer on the site of the Townhead flyover. The work was strenuous but it paid well. He could afford to rent a room from a lady called Elda who had agreed to attend to his laundry for a few extra shillings.

Gordon's apparent innocence and quiet nature had appealed to Elda and brought from her an uncharacteristic kindness and consideration. She had seen him as a country boy lost and alone in the big city. He had also felt sorry for her. She too was alone and all too frequently, drunk.

After a hard day's work Gordon Macrae would come home to his digs to find Elda asleep in a chair surrounded by empty screw-top beer bottles and half-bottles of vodka or gin. No meal would have been prepared and no washing done. He would simply shake his head and begin the work himself. When Elda eventually came round she would either apologise profusely or rage at Gordon for being so smart, depending on how much her sleep had sobered her.

Alison Henderson watched the ground drift downwards creating a large map for her to examine before the plane banked and her only view was a clear blue sky. She was just 19 years of age and she had never flown before. Already she liked the experience. It somehow epitomised exactly what she was doing in the summer of 1967.

She had begun Nursing Training at Glasgow's Southern General Hospital but had soon realised just how little her colleagues were being recognised and rewarded. The older nurses would never see a day when their wages rose to anything worthwhile. The type of person who became a nurse was not the kind to readily withdraw their labour and, for as long as that remained the case, there would be no improvement in their finances. When she had considered the working experience of the last few years and her current prospects, she could see little reason to continue. Glasgow was offering very little to a person like her. She wanted to improve matters at a personal level. Staying at home would mean constantly dumbing down, to a level below where she wanted to be, just to suit other people. She had no wish to remain immature and average. She had been attracted by nursing positions in the USA and Canada being explained by recruitment staff from these countries who were currently running a recruitment campaign in Glasgow for nurses and police officers. She had chosen New York and had seldom, if ever, felt this excited in her whole life.

Leaving her parents behind had been a real wrench. She had no way of knowing when she might see them again but they had been supportive of her decision. Her two older brothers had also given their blessing to her going. She must do her best in America to prove herself worthy of their trust and support.

The flight took almost six hours and for the most part there had been nothing to see other than white cloud far below and occasionally the sight of another aircraft, looking small and distant. She leaned back and closed her eyes.

A few moments later, alerted by the 'oohs' and 'aahs' of other passengers, she looked out her window to catch her first view of the Statue of Liberty looking magnificent in the sunlight. It seemed to be an omen, a welcoming omen for Nurse Alison Henderson to her future in New York.

Thomas Fraser was dressed in a suit, a felt hat and a gabardine raincoat. He looked no different from most Glasgow businessmen. He was certainly not one of them but he knew the benefits of mingling anonymously with the crowd. It was the lunch hour and he was not the only man visiting the large department store at lunchtime in the week before Christmas 1967. He purchased a cardigan for his sister-in-law and a jersey for his brother. The bag with the store name on it might be useful later. He had made two previous trips during this busy time of the day and now felt comfortable with his knowledge of the interior layout of the store. He had also watched the store closing in the early evening and had seen nothing to suggest that staff were conveying cash to the bank. He had spent the best part of Friday watching for any transfer from the store to a bank but there had been none. His intuition was seemingly correct where this particular store was concerned. It was still operating as it always had. The stone building, the fittings and furnishings, the lifts with their double gate entry and the carved plaster ceilings, too high to be dusted, all spoke of a bygone age. The business methods had not moved on either it seemed and security had not improved to deal with men like Thomas Fraser. He would return on Saturday afternoon, the last before Christmas.

Earlier that month he had gone to an unlit and remote stone quarry twelve miles north of the city. He had gone there during a Sunday night to steal detonators and fuse wire. It had taken much longer than he had expected and he had been forced to make a return trip the following Sunday night to break into the other magazine for the actual explosive.

On Saturday afternoon, with the department store at its busiest, Fraser joined the throng posing as yet another Christmas shopper. He was wearing his gabardine coat again but beneath it he had a boiler suit with pockets full of detonators, cordite and explosive. He had even packed a sandwich and a chocolate bar.

The main office was located on the second floor and Fraser had noticed a hollow wooden cube, painted white, which supported a mannequin in fancy clothing close to the office area. The open back of the cube faced the wall and was large enough to conceal Fraser if he chose his moment carefully to duck inside. Once there he was unlikely to be found. He waited some distance away for a safe opportunity. When others looked elsewhere he took his chance.

Towards six o'clock the store was falling silent and the few voices and footsteps seemed to belong to staff. He heard keys jangling on hoops and voices calling out 'Happy Christmas' and 'Have a good break'. Eventually Fraser saw that lights were being extinguished and the second floor was almost in complete darkness. He remained in the cube for another hour just in case someone had forgotten something or had a duty security round to do. He heard nothing.

He crept out of the box and stretched his legs. He was not a young man and with any luck this job would be his last. He walked to the office which comprised a walled off area of the floor with opaque glass panels on three sides risings upwards for about four feet from the wooden partition walls. The door was of a matching construction and was locked. Fraser took out a small torch and examined the door lock. It was a simple interior box lock. He took from his pocket a short length of thick wire that he bent into an 'L' shape to resemble a small hex key. He inserted this into the lock and with some patient twisting he managed to unlock the door. Ahead of him, beyond the large wooden desk, lay the old safe. He had glimpsed it earlier in the week as he walked around the floor watching staff come and go from the office. Donning a pair of rubber gloves, Fraser began to feel around the door of the safe and tried the central handle. It scarcely moved. Beneath the handle was a keyhole that would accept the safe key but would not permit the key to be inserted fully until it had been turned through 90 degrees. The proper means of entry was always best if it could be achieved and Fraser went to the manager's desk, another impressively constructed item. With his trusty wire he managed to unlock the top right hand drawer of the desk and found that this also released the drawers beneath it in the same pedestal.

There were keys but none that were suited to the safe. Entry would have to be by force after all. Fraser found that the keys he had would open the doors to all floors of the building and this would be of some help for upstairs, on the third floor, was the bed and bedding department. He would need mattresses and spent over an hour bringing every mattress that he could find down to the second floor. He filled the space around the safe with mattresses piled high from floor upwards until they covered the safe in an igloo shape. Only a small channel to the safe door was left. He would block that once he had prepared the safe for blasting. On the staircase of the third floor he had noticed a large metal plate which may have been a counterweight for the lift system. He found a handcart and with great difficulty he loaded the plate onto the cart.

He struggled manfully to lower the cart down the staircase and by the time he had reached the second floor his fingers had gone numb. He took the plate along to the office and tipped it against the front of the safe.

Fraser taped up his gelignite on the front of the safe door and inserted his fuses, ready wired. He shuffled the heavy plate as close as he could to the safe door and completed the mattress wall behind the plate. A check of his watch told him that it was only midnight and too early to blow the safe. Outside in the street there were occasional shouts so there were still people going about. There was plenty of time. He went to the kettle in the corner of the office and made himself a mug of tea. He took out his packed sandwich and sat down at the desk with his mug of tea.

It was around three-thirty in the morning when a dull boom broke the stillness of the night. If it caught anyone's attention, they would simply pause to wonder what they had just heard and where the sound had come from. Fraser himself listened in much the same way, waiting for any reaction from the street below. He would not risk looking out of the window but he had heard nothing. He crawled around to the safe over fragments of mattress cover. The metal plate had been thrown away from the safe and was now pinning down skeletal mattress springs on top of the desk. The mechanism behind the safe handle had remained intact but had been blown away from the door and the operating bars of the lock. This was exactly the result Thomas Fraser had anticipated. He had served many years in prison for safe-blowing but he was one of the best 'petermen' in the city of Glasgow. With his rubber gloves on his hands again he picked away the broken metal and units from inside the safe before loading bundled cash from the safe shelves into his store bag. He always savoured this part of the job and took his time to transfer the bundles of notes and bags of coins into his thick plastic bag.

The street outside was well lit but Fraser opened a rear window that allowed him access to the old metal fire escape. He had no fear of heights but the fire escape moved about in a way that worried him, especially in the pitch darkness to the rear of the building. With the plastic bag jammed under his coat he finally reached the ground and made his way through the streets, afraid that some patrolling police officer might emerge at any time. The only people he actually saw were milkmen and a lorry driver emptying skips.

He waited in the shadows at the top of a cul-de-sac, for daylight to arrive. He was frozen and tired but he knew that his brother and sister-in-law would be going to church that morning. As soon as he saw them leave the street he walked smartly down to their close and climbed the stone staircase to the top flat. He had a lot to do in the next hour.

Gordon Macrae, now working at the site of the new airport, had encouraged Elda to drink less. While he would reject any invitation from her to join her drinking sessions he would accept invitations to be with her on any sober outings she might suggest. Elda had listened with great interest to Gordon's anecdotes and reminiscences from his crofting days. The way he spoke had an enchanting effect on her. The life he described so honestly was a fairyland of simple pleasures. She was much more reticent and secretive where her own past was concerned. Gordon had sensed this and was certain that Elda had been a victim of a dark 'city life' in some sorry way.

Over time they had grown closer, more tolerant of their differences and failings until they eventually shared enough common ground as to see a future together. In 1968 they were married at the Registry Office. He was fifty-three and she was forty-three.

For George Prentice 1968 brought no such romance but it did provide him with company. The threat of violence from fellow prisoners had diminished but his own lack of personality had continued to ensure his unpopularity, even with the most sociable of convicts and staff. Prentice was silent except when ordered to speak and would have preferred to remain alone and silent. When required to speak his answers were brief.

In March of 1968 he was joined by 58 year old Thomas Fraser, a career criminal beginning a 12 year stretch for safe-blowing. With a serious list of previous convictions for similar crimes behind him, Fraser's sentence reflected some sympathy for his age. He had blown open a safe in the week before Christmas and had correctly imagined that the store takings would be a maximum amount. His sentence might have reflected even more sympathy if the stolen money had been recovered but every penny of the £12,332 remained unaccounted for. During police interview and at his trial Fraser had insisted that he had lost the bag containing the money by leaving it in a waste skip to avoid being seen with it in daylight. When he had returned on the Sunday night the skip had been emptied. The police had enquired into his account and found that skips in that area had been emptied early on Sunday morning making his account quite plausible. The circumstances of the case had been well covered in the press.

Despite his long criminal past, Fraser had never shown any tendency towards violence, in fact he was on record as being gentle and polite. He had never married and his crimes from his juvenile days had all been committed without accomplices. He was the 'thinking man's criminal' and an old hand at prison life. The prison authorities considered him appropriate company for George Prentice. The two men could ignore each other constantly, creating no problem for the staff.

For several weeks the men did live in silent co-existence just as predicted but gradually the ice between them began to crack. One would pass comment on something arising from that day and nothing more would be said. They both felt free to pass comment without expectation of a reply. Nothing contentious was ever said, simply a word or two of observation, but enough to provide the other man with an understanding of the feelings and opinions they might have in common. Legal counsel, medical attention, prison related interviews apart, neither of them received visits from outside, no friends, and no family. Tom Fraser had mentioned having a younger brother but had firmly stated that this brother would never visit Tom. It would be up to Tom to visit his brother when his release date came. Prentice told of his older sister and of how she would never want to see him in prison either.

The previous year had seen an increase in knife crime in Glasgow from the developing gang culture around the large housing estates, most notably Easterhouse. Convicted culprits had swelled the prison numbers with brash young men who were not prepared to be constrained by the prison system. George Fraser had no reason to see these young men as a threat but he followed the advice of Tom Fraser and other older cons to avoid eye contact with any of the young 'gang' crowd. The gang members were out to enhance their reputations for violence and would readily accept any staring as a challenge or excuse to make someone another victim.

A notice about available reading material had caught Prentice's eye and on his way from the dining hall he stopped to read it, aware of the footsteps passing behind him. In the same instinctive way he realised, all too late, that the footsteps had stopped and a group had formed at his back. He never saw any faces or heard any voices. There was no warning at all, just an intense pain in his side. He felt sick and faint as his legs failed to support him and he collapsed to the floor.

When he came round he was in a hospital bed with a prison officer seated on either side of him. He asked them what had happened and was told that he had been stabbed by someone. A sharpened coat hook had been found but nobody had seen the attack. That was what the prison officers told him, with little suggestion of sympathy or interest. What the doctors told him was more alarming. He had been three hours in surgery and the stab wound had come within millimetres of puncturing his heart. Had that happened he would never have made it to hospital in time to survive.

Prentice spent almost two weeks in hospital before being returned to the prison and Tom Fraser, the only man who had shown any pleasure in his company.

With each passing month Prentice and Fraser realised another shared reality; they both had several years to run before release. This seemed to bond them in a way that had not been foreseen. Fraser had a wealth of experience and had actually served during the war using his criminal skills in France together with new skills of forging false identities. Prentice was fascinated by these accounts and hung on his cell mate's every word as Fraser explained the arts he had used. He heard of simple but subtle forms of disguise, of how additional pockets could be sown into clothing in such a way as to escape attention during searches.

The two men were separated for a while with Fraser being transferred to Lowmoss Prison for a few months. He later returned to Barlinnie after posting a request to do so. He and Prentice were soon keeping company again with George Prentice gaining major benefit and prestige from the association. The older man was respected by convicts and staff alike as experienced and sensible. Prentice could never hope to emulate Fraser but stored up every item of advice and knowledge Fraser uttered. There were underlying differences in their characters and Prentice was instinctively aware of them. Fraser was a loner by design, Prentice was a loner by nature.

George Prentice never forgot what Fraser had said about his younger brother, a man who would not visit Tom in prison but someone Tom fully intended to visit when he got out. Prentice had no such feelings about visiting his sister if he was released. He just could not understand Fraser's attitude towards his brother. He waited until the conversation again raised the subject of visitors or, in their case, the lack of them.

"If your brother isn't prepared to visit you in prison, Tom, why would you go to see him once you got out?"

"Where else can I go?" Fraser had said immediately, spreading his hands as if the question required no thought.

"But he doesn't want you, Tom."

Fraser smiled.

"At one time he would have turned me away, George. Now that we are getting on a bit he would let me stay. He has taken me in before. I was staying with him the last time I got caught." he said, pausing to recall the event.

"The police went to your brother's house to get you?" Prentice asked.

"No really." Fraser answered with a chuckle. "Me and Arthur and his missis ran out into their arms you could say. It was that storm in the middle of January when the winds were that strong they blew down chimney breasts and everything. The wind was hellish strong and it blew big lumps of sandstone down through the roof of my brother's house. His house is a top flat and the concrete was coming in through the ceiling. We were out our beds like a shot and into the stairs. The sister-in-law was scared shitless man. We just ran down the stairs and the police were in the close at the bottom. They were in a' the closes in Partick tae stop folk running out into the street. The street was covered in boulders and slates, big lumps of wood and chimney pots. The cars in the street were wrecked and dustbins were flying down the road. Anyhow, the cop in our close recognised me and nabbed me for the store job. They must have twigged it was me that done it and that guy knew to look out for me." said Fraser with remorse in his voice. He now regretted having taken off his gloves to make himself a mug of tea.

"Will your brother be all right? I mean will he still be

staying there? Surely they would have to fix his house?" Prentice asked as if concerned.

"The council sorted his house. I know they did for my lawyer told me. Arthur will still be there if he is no away tae America." Fraser laughed as if he had just made a joke, one that he alone could appreciate.

"How would he do that?" Prentice asked flatly.

Tom Fraser stopped laughing and looked seriously at Prentice.

"It was aye something that Arthur wanted to do. He always talked about going tae America but he'll no go now. He is too old and his missis died in '74."

With that he looked up at the ceiling as if thinking more seriously. Prentice continued to look at him for several moments without speaking. For the time being and for reasons that were not entirely obvious this conversation had just ended.

No lasting damage had been done by this strange conversation but the subject of Tom Fraser's younger brother was not raised again for years. Both men also avoided any discussion or questions around the crimes for which Prentice had been imprisoned. Everyone knew about them and it served no purpose to talk about them. Tom Fraser had no fascination with violent crime. He had long resented the fact that convicted safe-blowers could expect to serve lengthy prison terms when the only person at risk of harm was themselves. Rapists and killers might receive similar sentences for inflicting terrible hurt to men, women or children. Where was the justice in that?

The blowing of safes was a magical and mystical operation for most criminals and Fraser continued to fill Prentice's head with tales of his exploits in his favourite criminal pastime.

"There will soon not be any safes left to blow." Tom told him. "They have had their day."

"How come?" Prentice asked.

"A lot of things tell me that, George. Folk are gonna be using more cheques instead of cash. The businesses don't want to be holding money any more. A lot of them are going to the banks in the afternoon with the bulk of their takings. The office safes are no gonna have the same money in them frae now on. I was just lucky to catch one of the old stores in the week afore Christmas when they were too busy tae go tae the bank."

"You were no all that lucky, Tom. You lost the money anyway and you got caught." Prentice said with a teasing smile.

"Aye right enough, George, but I'll no get caught again. When I get out o' here I'm gonna retire."

"You'll be out before me, Tom. Will you come and visit me in your retirement?" Prentice asked as if joking.

"Of course old son, I'll bring you a copy of my memoirs."

Alison Henderson was enjoying life in New York. Most of her friends were nursing staff and members of the medical profession but there were other people, in shops, cafes, burger stalls who formed part of her day with a ready smile and a cheery word. The city felt positive.

She had finished her training but wasn't satisfied to stand still. She heard how colleagues wanted to gain certain qualifications in line with future interests and she felt the same way. For her it was children. She could not imagine anything more fulfilling than helping seriously ill children to return to the happy young life they should be enjoying. How rewarding was that?

Through her spell in ER she had met a young doctor called Martin Swarbeck who had taken time to help her with her paediatric studies. Martin was also studying on his own account. He was aiming to become a paediatric surgeon and he tried to keep abreast of the latest biochemistry research. He was a serious young man and needed someone to help him relax. Alison was that girl. Their consultations by telephone, their meetings over coffee to discuss study topics or specific illnesses developed into walks in the park to assess developments in their hospital and the results of their respective examinations.

The casual arrangement continued and they gradually realised that a bond had been formed between them. This bond might have been more obvious but for the constraints of leisure time shared. Nothing had ever been a 'date' in the normal sense of the term. Usually it had been a realisation that a window was available to cover matters they had already scheduled for themselves in their separate quests for improvement. This had carried on for almost ten months and they could appreciate that life together would always be this demanding whatever their relationship.

Alison had gone with her paediatric drive and had become, from a nursing perspective, quite an authority on child healthcare. Martin had suggested to her in all seriousness that she should take a degree course. Alison had been enthusiastic but felt that she would be neglecting children in order to benefit personally. Four years without children seemed less of an option.

Martin was not like-minded. He was prepared to take on whatever was necessary to bolster his career and he advanced professionally pretty much as he wished.

In 1975, at the age of twenty-eight, Martin Swarbeck achieved his aim of becoming a paediatric surgeon. Nobody was more proud of Martin than Alison, with the possible exception of two parents who came up from Virginia to celebrate with him.

Martin invited Alison to join him and his parents for dinner at a well-known restaurant. When the meal was over and in the presence of parents who had only known Alison for the duration of the meal, Martin Swarbeck proposed, right there at the table. He even produced an expensive engagement ring. His choice was not entirely random for he and Alison had joked over rings at a jewellers' shop window one day, ages before. He had obviously been holding back until he made surgeon. If that was his style, she liked it.

They were married later that year and chose a small church near Martin's birthplace in Virginia. Alison's parents and brothers travelled from Scotland to attend. The sun shone on her that day, just as it had on the Statue of Liberty when she had first arrived in New York.

The sun continued to shine as the couple honeymooned around Virginia Beach but Alison claimed not to have noticed. In a cheeky postcard to her parents she remarked that 'the ceilings are so lovely in Virginia'.

Life for Alison seemed to have been fulfilled the following spring when she learned that she was expecting a child. Martin was equally delighted. He felt entirely capable of providing for a family and realised the joy that the news had meant to Alison. His normal stoic ability to conceal his emotions failed him on a few occasions. When this happened he could depend on his wife to tease him.

He noticed how his wife's feelings towards the children of others had not diminished following the news of her own happy condition. Alison still cried over the death of some poor child she could have done nothing to prevent. She still rejoiced over the seemingly miraculous recovery of others. Martin Swarbeck was proud of his wife and her love, more genuine than professional, for the gift of children.

Little Emma arrived on the 12th of September 1976 after eighteen hours of labour. Exhausted though she was, Alison insisted that Martin make everyone aware of how well she and Emma were following the birth.

A week later from her own telephone at home, she was able to repeat the exercise. For the first two years of Emma's life her mother spent every day with her. Gradually Emma was introduced to a good friend of her mother's, a nurse from nursery care who was known well enough to be trusted with Emma. Alison was ready to resume work. Her baby was bright and lively. There were no health issues to worry Alison and she felt privileged to be able to return to the paediatric unit.

In the early weeks of 1980 Tom Fraser smiled almost constantly. He joked about being able to smell the 'fresh Partick air' and wondering if he could scrape together enough money to watch 'the Thistle'. The old man was due for release and Prentice could only look on with envy as other cons wished Tom 'all the best' and kidded him about how much they would miss him. The subject would be raised as the men stood in line to 'slop out', the time honoured practice of dispensing of one's human waste into a real toilet from a personal waste bucket.

While standing in this queue Tom Fraser suddenly gripped his left arm with his right hand just before falling sideways to the floor. His waste bucket spilled onto the floor beside him. Anxious calls went out to staff and soon Tom was on board a stretcher heading for sick bay. His face was chalky white and his eyes had remained shut. George Prentice felt stunned. Had he just lost his only friend?

Word spread around the prison that Tom had come round in the sick bay and had been seen by a doctor. He would remain in sick bay for the time being.

"Any chance I could see him?" Prentice asked the surly officer, aware that he had never spoken voluntarily to the man before. The prison officer looked at him in silence for a few moments before responding.

"That depends if he wants to see you."

"That's fair enough. Could you ask?" Prentice pleaded. The officer merely nodded and walked away.

Two days later, in the afternoon, the surly guard came to Prentice's cell and told him to accompany him to the sick bay. Tom Fraser had improved and would be transferred to hospital. He had asked to speak to Prentice before he went.

Tom Fraser managed a smile when he saw Prentice. Still looking pale and feeble he raised a hand from the bedclothes and Prentice grasped the thin cold fingers.

"How are you doing, Tom. You gave me a bit of a fright."

"Suppose I did," Fraser said huskily. "Got a bit of a fright mysel'. They tell me it was a heart attack and quite a bad one at that." His voice was quiet and croaking. "I'm goin' tae the hospital, George, did they tell you that?"

"Aye, they did. That's why I'm here. I know they'll not let me see you in hospital so I asked to see you afore you went. I will just be sitting in here and wondering how you are getting on."

At this point the prison guard had stepped outside the open door to converse with a colleague. Tom Fraser raised his free hand to interrupt Prentice.

"I've written a letter tae Arthur, my brother," he said in a forced whisper. "If anything happens tae me would ye see that he gets it? It's in my drawer." He turned his head towards the bedside cabinet.

George Prentice could see that Fraser was taking advantage of the moment and the opportunity it presented to pass his letter without the guard knowing. He moved closer to the cabinet and pulled the drawer open enough to insert his hand and pull out a small envelope, all the while looking at Fraser. He closed the drawer and held the envelope in front of himself where Fraser could see it. The older man gave an almost imperceptible nod, Prentice pushed the envelope inside his shirt.

"I'll just hold on to it, Tom. You'll be back in a week or two, brand new and ready to hit the road. The hospital will sort you, wait and see."

Tom Fraser smiled and winked.

"I hope you're right George. If you're wrong it's been a pleasure knowing you."

The prison officer stepped back into the room.

"Right Prentice, you've had your five minutes. It's time for you to leave. That's the ambulance arrived for Fraser."

Prentice returned to his cell and lay on his bed for a full ten minutes thinking about Tom Fraser. He purposefully avoided looking towards the peep-hole in the door for he could expect the guard to look for any unusual activity after a visit to sick bay. Only when he felt reasonably free to move about did he rise and lift the book he had been reading. He opened it onto his stomach, as if reading it. His free hand slowly pulled the envelope from his shirt and placed it in the open book. Now it would not be seen by any peeping guard. The envelope was sealed but Arthur Fraser's address was on the front. Prentice smiled as he read the address. He knew the street in Partick and he could visualise exactly where Arthur Fraser's flat would be. The envelope was light and the letter obviously brief. Prentice unrolled several sheets of toilet roll until only the cardboard core remained. He wrapped the letter around the core and patiently rewound the toilet paper until the roll again looked to be intact and not the least bit suspicious.

For almost a week there was no news of Fraser but one morning two officers came to the cell and asked Prentice to identify which personal items belonged to Fraser and which to himself. It was quite obvious that Fraser was not coming back to the cell, but why? Prentice asked the question and was informed that Tom Fraser had passed away in hospital during the night.

Prentice sat on his bed stunned by the news, nodding in response to officer's questions.

"Has anyone told his brother?" Prentice asked thoughtfully.

"His brother was his next of kin. The hospital got in

touch with him apparently." was the solemn reply before both officers left with their list and Fraser's few possessions in a cardboard box. Tom had not owned much in that cell but to Prentice the place seemed bigger and emptier. He lay back on his bed feeling sorry for old Tom, but even sorrier for himself. Rolling himself a cigarette with tobacco he had plundered from Tom's tin before the older man had gone to hospital, Prentice thought about the change of circumstances. Old Tom had been due to leave and probably stay with his brother in Partick. It would be another two years before Prentice would be released. He had hoped that old Tom would have been there to help and advise him, just like always. Now there would be no Tom to do that, nobody and nothing to help him, he thought, as his eyes turned towards the toilet roll. Perhaps there was a way.

In 1980 Gordon Macrae reached the age of sixty-five. He had managed to remain in continuous employment although his work had passed from labouring to warehouse work for a DIY chain. He had invested in endowment plans and savings designed to provide some financial security when he retired. He was happy at work but had always held the wish to spend his retirement years in a highland setting, if not Sutherland, at least somewhere of natural highland beauty. He expected to encounter some difficulty in tempting Elda to join him in his wish, leaving behind her precious Glasgow. It was the city of her birth and her life thereafter. She had spent her whole life in the city.

There was an East Kilbride tour company that ran short holiday trips to the highland towns. Would she give it a try? He asked her and was pleasantly surprised when she agreed. She was a different woman from the old Elda nowadays. She had become a dutiful housewife who could be relied upon to cook good meals and clean her home thoroughly. She made the point that one of these highland tours would take her away from her domestic work for a week.

In the course of their week away, Gordon hoped to persuade Elda of the virtue of his ideas on retirement. The holiday would oblige her into the capacity of a captive audience but his wife was a Glasgow woman after all. If she did not like the idea of moving out of the city she would soon tell him. He was encouraged by her silence.

As they strolled around the streets of Corran Bay, looking in shop windows, they stumbled on an estate agents' window. The firm was offering a letting service and it was there, in one of the glossy photographs, that they first saw the cottage for let on Lauradale Estate. The monthly rental amounted to £36 more than their current rent in Glasgow. With a little coaxing Gordon convinced Elda that they should go in and enquire on the property and the terms of any lease. There were further photographs to show the interior and the improvements brought about by the estate owner, Gregor Mackay. The girl in the office told them that they ought to act quickly if they liked the cottage. It was attractive and the busy holiday season would bring interest. There was another smaller cottage on the estate due for refurbishment but this one was ready and right in the public eye. Anyway, the second cottage would not be as attractive even when refurbished. They expressed their interest and left the office with photographs in a brochure and the business card for the agency stapled to a list of terms and conditions for tenancy.

Gordon was delighted to have found such a place. He could now talk to Elda on the basis of something they both knew about. A peaceful country cottage, one that might have been received with scorn as being a pipedream, was actually there within their grasp. He tried to convince her that fate was playing a hand. She became pensive. For her such a change represented a much greater step than it did for Gordon and the poignancy of the name of the estate had not escaped her.

By the time they returned to Glasgow they had decided that they could live out their retirement at Lauradale. Gordon withdrew the amount required as a deposit to secure the rental and posted it off to the letting agency with a letter confirming their wish to become tenants.

TWO

At Lauradale Estate the Macraes settled in quickly and any fears Gordon had expected for Elda being too isolated were assuaged by the kindliness of Laura Mackay. She had been a Glasgow girl too with a background and family not unlike that of Elda. The two women found in each other a link to their younger days and from the outset considered each other to be a friend.

Laura Mackay had no airs or graces but it was evident that she was enjoying a more comfortable, even luxurious, lifestyle than Elda Macrae. She had been a single mother in Aberdeen, working as an agency typist when she had the good fortune to meet Gregor Mackay. He was a Texan and already in an executive position with an oil company conducting exploration work in the North Sea. He was considered to be a hard man to please and Laura had seen signs of that in him, but none of his anger was ever directed at her. She would have told him where to get off and he always seemed to sense that. He also admired her temperament and confidence.

He had taken Laura out to dinner and told her about the unpleasant marriage he had left behind in Texas. His divorce was going through the court as they spoke. He expected that it would cost him much more than it should but it would make him free again. He had invited Laura to lay her cards on the table and hide nothing from him. She had struck him as being capable of that.

"Decisions can only ever be considered on the basis of honestly portrayed facts" was his motto, so he had told her, as if no-one should live without a motto.

Laura had told him of Lorna, her little daughter. There had never been a marriage and the girl's father had never known she existed. Laura was happy to keep things that way but looked directly at Gregor as she told him. She knew it was not a selling point for any potential suitor but Lorna was not negotiable.

Gregor returned her directness and nodded without saying anything. Laura had expected matters to end there with her disclosure, they normally would. Why would a wealthy Texas oilman find any attraction in a 24 year old single mother from Aberdeen with a twenty-four months old baby daughter?

Gregor Mackay never stated any objection or criticism, he simply remained silent on the topic of romantic interest. His divorce was not yet final.

When he received notification of his divorce being granted he asked Laura to join him for a celebratory meal. She accepted. She also accepted his invitations on subsequent evenings and over a period of time Laura felt that Gregor had no adverse feelings towards her situation.

If he had he would have dumped her by now. In conversation Gregor had made it clear that he was happy to accept Laura and her little girl. So soon after his divorce he was in no rush to commit to a future, even one that he wanted. That had been his version of 'honestly portrayed facts'. Laura had sensed that Gregor was not afraid of asking, he was just afraid of being rejected. He was not someone who accepted the word 'no' from anyone. He would have to be sure of her answer. It was not beyond the capabilities of a Glasgow lass like Laura to de-mist his vision.

They had married in the summer of the following year and honeymooned around the Western Isles. Lorna had stayed with her maternal grandparents for the duration of the honeymoon but on Gregor and Laura's return all three had moved into the Turnbull's large bungalow, at least until their own bungalow was completed.

Gregor had ensured that Laura Turnbull could become Mrs Laura Mackay and a few months later Lorna Turnbull legally became Lorna Mackay.

The bright young Lorna had grown to be a clever teenager, Laura told Elda. She began to study economics at Aberdeen University. That had created the opportunity for the Mackays to find a place for themselves in the country – Lauradale Estate.

Elda Macrae had always been reticent regarding her own life and led Laura Mackay to believe that she had no family and had simply been fortunate to 'find' Gordon. Of Gordon, Elda could speak freely.

Laura Mackay would not argue over the fine qualities of the man but she expected that a large story was not being told where Elda was concerned. Laura knew instinctively that the missing part would be interesting. She hoped to elicit more in good time.

Elda required no such patience with Laura Mackay. Laura talked easily about her life as Mrs Mackay, of how Gregor had found an estate called Lauradale and just had to buy it for their tenth wedding anniversary. He had also purchased a holiday bungalow in Florida to provide an escape from Scottish winters.

Elda listened with some fascination but could not really envy Laura. All things considered, Elda accepted that she had been fortunate to be living in a cottage on Lauradale Estate with Gordon Macrae for a husband.

The elderly couple in the front garden of their bungalow home in Aberdeen also considered themselves fortunate as they mowed the lawn and trimmed the shrubs.

The summer sun of 1982 shone down on the efforts of George and Fiona Turnbull as they maintained the beauty and neatness of the garden they had tended for over twenty years. Former employment in the oil industry and present retirement were things that George had in common with many of his neighbours in that quiet residential street.

Their home had once been home to their daughter and granddaughter too but then Gregor Mackay had married

Laura and adopted Lorna, bringing a satisfactory close to a less wonderful episode in their early lives.

A strange face was an unusual sight in the street but the unshaven individual in the ill-fitting suit and spectacles was certainly a stranger. He carried a small leather suitcase as if hoping to find accommodation somewhere. The Turnbulls were not the only residents to be at work in their gardens but the stranger took no notice of other people, only them. He slowed perceptibly as he reached the Turnbulls house and he stared at both George and Fiona Turnbull before looking at their car, parked in their driveway. He looked next at the house number displayed on a plate fixed to the front wall. He had never looked like speaking and he had not actually stopped walking but the Turnbulls had obviously held an interest for him. He passed by and continued down the street without paying any further attention to any house or person. George Turnbull watched him as he went. There was something sinister in the man's interest in the retired couple and their home.

"Did you see that chap that just walked past here?" George asked his wife who was weeding around some bedding plants.

"The one with the suitcase?" Fiona asked unnecessarily.

"Yes, he looked a bit odd."

"He looked a bit familiar too," Fiona said quietly, "but don't ask me why."

The other cottage on Lauradale Estate lay two hundred

yards from the Macraes, through undergrowth and over a substantial stream. Work was continuing there but the Macraes only heard the sound of work, they never saw the workmen. There was no direct path from one cottage to the other, in fact the cottages had entirely separate access roads. The access road past 'the big house' belonging to the Mackays continued to the left until it reached the Macrae cottage. The small cottage under renovation had its own access road from the public road.

Two years after the Macraes had moved in, the small cottage was deemed to be finished and it was advertised in the window of the same letting agency.

When the advertisement was removed from the window later in 1982, Gordon enquired with Laura Mackay as to whether a tenant had been found for it.

"I believe so, Gordon, a man called Fraser from Glasgow. He's about forty-three years of age apparently. I've not seen him yet" she replied without sounding particularly interested.

Over the following months it seemed to the Macraes that the new tenant was someone they would never get to see. He had to be staying there, they believed, for someone was burning the log fire. Every day smoke would rise above the bushes from the stainless steel stack.

Laura Mackay had told Elda during the summer that the man in the small cottage had asked Gregor if he could install central heating. He had insisted that he would be able to do it himself but Gregor had told him to forget the idea unless he was prepared to pay a professional firm to do the job.

"You know he is a creepy guy, Elda." Laura had said. "If I am out in my garden I get that feeling that somebody is watching me from the trees across the burn. One time I actually saw him. He had binoculars up to his eyes and he was not looking at me but at our Lorna. She was home from the university at the time. I never told Gregor. He would be furious."

After the Mackays had flown out to Florida and Gordon was left in charge of 'the big house', Elda suggested that they make a point of meeting the man in the other cottage.

"I think we should know what he looks like, Gordon, even if he doesn't want to meet us." she had suggested.

"We'll go round there sometime, Elda." Gordon had said with little enthusiasm. "Until then he is causing us no harm."

Andrew Fleming was a police officer who had always been interested in following up on reports of sudden death. He was not morbid or ghoulish, he simply wanted to ensure that matters were as they appeared. If this was the end of someone's life then it was worth his full attention. A sudden or unexplained death was all too often the name given to a death case before anyone had seen anything to prove that everything was as simple and natural as it was said to be. Even in police procedure 'sudden death' implied that someone had collapsed and died. In the use of codes the police had given a code to a 'sudden death' which delivered a preconceived notion that the death was perfectly natural. Why would an elderly person not die? After an enquiry that never tried to open any cans of worms, the report would often end with a conclusion to the effect that there were no suspicious circumstances. Fair enough, if the enquiring officer had actually looked for any and the enquiring officer should always look, according to Fleming. The dead person would want that and in these cases the deceased was the client. A rich man losing his fortune could never be compared to a poor man losing his life, even if both acts were criminal.

It was a cold January day in 1985 when Fleming drove north with his friend and colleague, Hamish MacLeod, to an estate lodge cottage following a report of such a death. A poor man had seemingly died while alone.

On his way he considered again how awkward these deaths could be. The only person known to have been present was the now deceased.

Eventually the officers reached a low-walled entrance where a wooden sign above the wall told them that they had reached 'Lauradale'. "We should be going left immediately we go through this entrance." Hamish reminded Fleming. "Straight ahead leads to the estate house. According to Charlie the owners stay there and they reported it." Charlie Macdonald was the office controller and he knew the area better than most.

Fleming turned left onto a little used single road where

the Land Rover forced its way through some overhanging branches and protruding gorse until a small cottage came into view beneath tall fir trees. In the shadow of the trees the cottage looked cold, damp and dark. Outside the cottage stood an elderly man wearing a deerstalker hat and leaning on a long stick with a carved ram's horn handle. He looked fit for his age. Fleming stopped the car. As the police officers approached the man he introduced himself.

"I am Gordon Macrae. I look after this place when the owners are away." He pointed towards the cottage door. "The man inside was a tenant. He has been staying here for the last two years or so but I've hardly seen much of him. I stay over there." He pointed his stick in the direction of his cottage and the police officers could see enough of a roof gable to suggest that another cottage stood two hundred yards away. "We are on the other side of a burn and we have no call to be coming round this way." Macrae explained.

"So what did bring you round here?" Fleming asked.

"This is January and for the past three months Mr Fraser has been burning his log fire every day. We can see the smoke from our house. It was pretty cold again this morning but there was no smoke from his fire. At first I wondered if he had run out of wood and we could have helped with that but his store of wood is fairly full. It would do him a while yet. Then I wondered if he might have gone away somewhere so I tried his door expecting it to be locked but it opened for me. Maybe he was ill, the man, so I went in. It looks like he has had a bit of an accident."

Gordon Macrae was already walking towards the cottage door and the police officers followed him in.

In the tiny lounge lay the body of a man who looked younger than Gordon Macrae, a man in his forties, perhaps. The body lay face down with the head towards the right side of the fireplace. An old armchair sat to the left of the fireplace, angled to face fire and ahead of it the grate held wood ash from which a poker extended out towards the armchair.

The 'accident' that Macrae had alluded to seemed have been the toppling of a heavy wooden unit which belonged against the right wall but had fallen on top of the body. The height of this unit would be about six feet or thereby, indicated by the pale square shadow on the painted wall. The upper half of the unit served as a bookcase and Fleming noticed how the books lay in overlapping fashion against the man's body. There was an open head wound in the back of the man's head where he could have been struck by the protruding outer edge of the ornamental beading around the top of the furniture unit. This wound had bled out to form a large pool on the floor making death from the head wound a distinct possibility.

As Hamish produced his notebook and began to note down Gordon Macrae's particulars, Fleming moved towards the wall where the unit had presumably stood for some length of time. The cleaner, paler outline on the wall included a small dent, about 2 inches in length and pointing downwards in a 'V' shape. The bottom of the 'V' bit into the plaster and the torn edges of old wallpaper looked to be bearing traces of deep red staining.

"Have you moved anything since you arrived, Mr Macrae?" he asked without suggesting that he had any particular reason for asking.

"No. I just saw what we see here. I checked to ensure he was dead but I already knew. I've seen this type of thing all too often before." His tone was regretful, not boastful.

"During the war?" Fleming guessed.

Macrae merely nodded in confirmation.

Fleming had moved to the fireplace where he removed the poker from the ashes and looked closely at the pointed head of the heavy poker. It was thicker and heavier than the shaft. Why would the dead man have left it in the fire? The ashes were cold and from the day before.

Hamish asked Macrae what he knew about the deceased. Did he work? Did he have family? How did he come to be here?

"I'm sorry to say I don't know him at all well." Macrae said, rubbing his chin with his hand as he spoke. I doubt that he was working when he could keep his fire burning all day. I never saw any visitors coming to the place other than the local chap that brings his logs. He sometimes goes to town by bus but usually he just goes to the village shop."

"How do you know his name? Do you know where he came from?" Hamish pressed.

"Not really. He arranged his tenancy through the estates agency in town. It was Gregor who told me his name."

"Who is Gregor?"

"Gregor Mackay. He is the owner of the estate. He owns this cottage and mine and the 'big house' of course."

"Did he know this man?" Hamish asked.

"I doubt that Gregor has spoken much to this man either but he once told me that the new tenant was an Arthur Fraser from Glasgow. The letting agency could have told him that just by passing on the papers. The boss will have them in his files, I dare say."

"Is the boss, Mr Mackay, at home?" Fleming asked, picking up on the need for early identification of the deceased.

"No. The Mackays have a house in Florida. They went there in October and I don't expect them back until March." Macrae said. "Mind you, Gregor is flying back at the end of this month. He is in the oil business and has to be in Aberdeen during February on business."

"Do you have access to the Mackay house, Mr Macrae?"

"Yes. I have the keys while they are away. I make sure that the heating is on and I collect the mail. You will be thinking about the files I mentioned but I have no key to them."

Fleming was still looking about the walls of the cottage. "No telephone?"

"Not that I know of."

Just then a vehicle stopped outside and Gordon Macrae moved to the window.

"That will be the doctor, Mr Macrae. He has seen a lot of death too and only when he says that this man is dead can we hope to remove the body. I would ask you to leave us while we speak to the doctor, Mr Macrae, but before you leave us I must ask you if you knocked over that stool?"

To the right of the fallen unit lay a three-legged milking stool.

"No. I was never near it, officer." Macrae said solidly before ducking out the door of the cottage.

The doctor carried out a cursory examination of the body and thought it quite likely that the head wound had been the cause of death. He stood upright and looked at the body and the fallen unit in turn.

"Yes boys, life extinct, as they say. It looks like an accident but what exactly was this poor bugger doing?"

Fleming and MacLeod laughed.

"That is the question that we must find an answer for, doctor."

Fleming accompanied the doctor out to where the vehicles were parked. As the doctor drove away the police officer radioed for the CID to attend at the cottage.

While waiting for the CID, Fleming and MacLeod

moved about the cottage without disturbing anything. The bedroom was like the other rooms, tidy and functional. The bedroom smelled slightly of dampness but the house was clean and well kept. The bed was made ready for use and did not look slept-in. At the bottom corner of the top cover pyjamas lay folded. The way this house was being kept made Fleming wonder if the dead man had been a soldier. There was a discipline involved here. The bedroom had a fireplace but the grate and hearth were clean, suggesting that it had not been in use for a long time. A three bar electric fire sat in the hearth with a lead plugged into a nearby socket.

"Somebody meant something to the guy." Hamish remarked, pointing to a photograph beside the bed. The black and white photograph was only 5 inches by three and showed a teenage girl in a white dress. Behind her other people, out of focus, were dancing. The snapshot was held in a 10 by 8 inch frame. Fleming studied the photograph without touching it.

"I wonder who you are, young lady?" he asked. "You must be important to Mr Fraser, you are the only picture in his house."

Beside the photo frame on the bedside cabinet was a pair of spectacles, a tobacco tin and an old saucer which served as an ashtray. In the saucer, among the ash, there were cigarette ends, each less than an inch long and as thin as matchsticks.

"Our man has been in the Bar-L, Hamish. Tobacco is

the currency in prison and they soon learn to roll their cigarettes this thin."

A few minutes later the CID arrived in the form of Detective Sergeant Douglas Campbell and Detective Constable Darren Black. Fleming pointed out the discrepancies to the idea of a self-inflicted accident.

"Like the doctor said, Dougie, what was the guy doing? It looks as if the unit fell on him but could he cause that? His feet are farther from the unit than his head is."

"He could have fallen from the top of the unit to the floor and then had the unit fall on him while he was trying to get to his feet." Campbell suggested slowly as if not convinced by his own suggestion.

"I don't think the unit caused his injury." Fleming said confidently. "The top edge of the unit is clean and it is four inches from that wound at its nearest point."

"So, if not the unit, then what hit the guy on the head?" Campbell asked.

"I think it was the poker, Dougie." Fleming said with the same confidence, pointing to the poker, now lying in the hearth. "Just imagine that man walking into this room. He has to come through this door and head in the direction his body is pointing now. If struck from behind then he falls to the position he is in now."

"Fair enough." said Campbell, "But what about the unit? Why pull it over?"

"To give the impression of an accident." Fleming answered. "You are the third person to suggest immediately that the falling unit could have killed this man."

"The unit is heavy enough, just look at all these books. It must have weighed a ton." Campbell argued.

"Exactly." Fleming responded. "Whoever pulled it over had to stand on that stool to gain the leverage to pull it down. The stool is on its side and I'm guessing that the person fell for these stools are not really for standing on. Do you see that dent in the plaster behind the unit? It is fresh and I think I see blood at the edges. When we came in here that poker was stuck in the ashes of the fire. Who would do that?"

"Put there while the fire was still alight?" Darren Black suggested.

"No point in looking for blood on the poker then." Campbell commented. "Okay Andy, who reported this?"

"Gordon Macrae. He stays in the house over behind this one. He claims to scarcely know this man on the floor but he had noticed that the daily fire had not been lit and came round to see what might be wrong. The estate owner is Gregor Mackay but he and his family are away in Florida. He won't be back until the end of the month. The dead man is said to be an Arthur Fraser from Glasgow. The estates letting agency apparently have documentary proof of this."

"Okay Andy, I'll get this lot dusted and photographed. Better put the undertaker on stand-by. I'll go round to the Macraes when I'm done here."

Fleming and MacLeod left and returned to the office by way of the estates letting agency.

There they were shown photocopies of documents used by the now deceased, Arthur Fraser, for identification; an old driving licence and an extract birth certificate. Fleming requested and received additional photocopies of these. He was told by the clerk in the office that photocopies had also been given, together with completed rental agreements, to Mr Gregor Mackay. The annual rent had been paid in advance plus a deposit against damages. Payments had been in cash. Leaving his photocopies at the office with Hamish he headed back to the cottage to await the undertakers. Hamish prepared an initial report on the death.

When Detectives Campbell and Black had completed their examination of the cottage and the body had been removed for post mortem, the CID drove round to the Macraes' cottage.

Gordon Macrae introduced his wife Elda and sat beside his wife. She remained silent but attentive.

He related the story of Fraser asking permission to install a central heating system in the cottage, a request that Mackay had refused when he learned that Fraser meant to do the work personally.

Gordon Macrae again explained how the smoke from Fraser's chimney had indicated his presence every day until that morning when there was no smoke. There had still been no fire an hour later and that had been sufficiently unusual for Macrae to have investigated. He had found things in the cottage to be just as the officers had seen the place. He had checked for life signs but touched nothing else.

"How long has Arthur Fraser lived there?" Campbell asked.

"Just over two years. Before that the house was empty. The Mackays had done some work on it to make it habitable so we never knew anyone else who might have lived there." Macrae replied.

"Have you seen much of him?"

The Macraes looked at each other. Again it was Gordon who spoke.

"Not really. We have only seen him from a distance, even in the summer months. The layout of this estate makes us farther apart than you might think. We only really met him at New Year, just three weeks ago. We felt like we had been poor neighbours so we walked round on the second of January just to say 'Hello' and invite him to call on us if he ever needed anything. He was very quiet and ..."

" ... and a bit weird." Elda Macrae finished the sentence for her husband.

"In what way was he weird, Mrs Macrae?" Campbell asked.

"He never really spoke. We did all the talking. He never said more than two or three words at a time and he looked nervous all the time." she explained. "His eyes would never really look at you. When he spoke he looked down or away. To my mind he either had mental problems or something to hide."

"That was at New Year, you said. Did you or he have any drink on that occasion?"

"No, we took a bottle of sherry round with us but he wasn't interested and we don't drink much nowadays. We left the bottle with him actually."

"So you visited but learned very little about the man. Have either of you gone back to the cottage for any reason since? Apart from this morning, I mean."

"No." Elda Macrae said quite emphatically.

"She doesn't like him." Gordon explained. "He seemed to avoid looking at Elda when we were there, just like she said. Whether he was afraid of women, or just Elda, we'll never know but that was what it looked like."

"Did he have a good fire burning when you visited him?" Darren Black asked with a smile.

"Yes he did." Gordon confirmed.

"Not as good as the one he has now." Elda remarked without humour.

After an awkward moment of silence Douglas Campbell asked Gordon Macrae if he knew when Gregor Mackay would be home.

"His flight comes into Glasgow on Sunday morning. He intends to hire a car and use it to go to Aberdeen the next day." was Gordon's answer.

"So I can hope to catch him here on Sunday afternoon?"

"I expect so."

When Campbell and Black returned to Lauradale on Sunday 27th January they knew that Gregor Mackay was home. A new Ford car sat near to the front door. Nothing on the vehicle said 'car rental' but there was no need.

As the two detectives left their own vehicle they heard the sound of raised voices from within the house. The softer voice belonged to Gordon Macrae and the other louder, angrier voice had to be that of Gregor Mackay. Campbell knocked on the front door and then heard the loud footsteps of someone strutting to respond.

The door was pulled open forcefully and a heavily set man with a red complexion and wild eyes looked out on Campbell and Black.

"Who are you?" he asked, his tone quite unwelcoming.

"CID. I am Detective Sergeant Campbell and my colleague is Detective Constable Black. We are here to speak with Mr Gregor Mackay concerning the death of Arthur Fraser."

"Arthur Fraser? Who the hell is Arthur Fraser?"

"He had the lease of the small cottage." Gordon Macrae said softly from several feet behind Mackay.

"Oh, of course, I see," Mackay said almost apologetically. "I am Gregor Mackay. You had better come in. I think we may have a lot to talk about."

With that he turned on his heel and stormed back into

his front room where Macrae was told, "This is not the end of the matter, Gordon. I dare say these men will want to speak to you later. I expect you to be at home when they call."

Macrae looked at Mackay with disdain but resisted the temptation to tell him what to do with his expectations.

"I'll be there." he said firmly. "But only because I choose to be." With that he walked out past the two CID men.

"I'm sorry to be this angry gentlemen but who wouldn't be angry after three hours driving to reach home only to find that my favourite painting has been stolen." Mackay said resentfully, throwing himself down into a large armchair. His accent was decidedly American.

"Was it a valuable painting?" Campbell asked.

"Yeah, I suppose it was. Some guy called Samuel Peploe had painted a stretch of beach on Skye. My wife and I were there on honeymoon in '65. I saw the painting going to auction and made sure I got it. I gave it to Laura as a birthday present. She's gonna be heartbroken when she learns it's gone."

"Can we deal with the death of Arthur Fraser first, Mr Mackay, then we can get all the details needed for the theft of your painting?" Campbell suggested.

Mackay nodded his agreement.

"I never really knew the guy. I spoke to him when he had been in the cottage a couple of days. I had got the place tidied up, new bedding, bathroom towels and so on.

DEATH OF A DEAD MAN

I had logs delivered for his fire and I asked if there was any more that he needed. He asked if he could install a central heating system to work from the log fire. He wanted to do this himself, you understand, no plumbers or heating engineers. I told him not to bother. He could leave it the way it was or employ a proper firm to do it at his expense. Any changes of the kind he was proposing, done by him and he could leave the tenancy. He would forfeit his deposit too. He accepted things the way they were. One way and another we never really met or spoke again. He never spoke to my wife either but she has apparently told her father that the guy was watching her through binoculars anytime she was outside in the garden, especially if Lorna was there."

"Lorna?" Campbell enquired.

"My daughter, she's twenty-two. She'll come home here in March when my wife comes back from the States."

"Did you have any documents on Arthur Fraser? Any background information?" Campbell asked.

"Only what the letting agency gave me. It's in my filing cabinet in the office." Mackay said, rising from his chair. "Follow me."

He walked smartly across the hall to the room opposite, which the officers found to be furnished with antique bookcases, wall mirrors and a huge leather top desk. Sharing the space in equal measure were devices of modern technology, computers, printers, fax machines and copiers. On the wall there hung a wide screen with wires running down to a camera aimed at the desk. Three large filing cabinets stood against the side wall with a fourth in the corner to the right of the bay window. As the men approached this corner cabinet Mackay pointed to the side wall overlooking the filing cabinet.

"That was where my picture hung, gentlemen. It was there when I left." he said with his annoyance still apparent.

Campbell had noticed the burglar alarm system fittings around what they had so far seen of the house and wondered how much pleasure Mrs Mackay could derive from her painting's location. He also wondered if the value to Gregor Mackay was not entirely sentimental. Laura's painting was his painting, he had just said so. Meanwhile Gregor Mackay was trying to fit a small key into the lock of the filing cabinet and was finding some difficulty in doing so. Campbell moved closer to look at the lock.

"Was it always this awkward?" he asked.

"Nope, in fact it was real easy. I think someone has damaged it."

"But nobody else uses it, do they?" Campbell asked as he bent to look along the edge of the top drawer.

"Nobody else has a key." Mackay confirmed.

"Was the edge always sticking out at this end?" Campbell asked, inviting Mackay to look at the edge as he had just done.

"I see what you mean. No, this drawer was as good as

new and fully closed. Now the lock don't work right and the drawer is buckled." Mackay said hopelessly.

"I don't think that anyone has actually managed to break into this cabinet, Mr Mackay, but someone has tried. Is there anything important inside?"

"Naw, that's why it's over here. It has the files for this estate house and the two cottages. Tenancy, repairs, insurance cover, nothing to break in for. My real business stuff is in these other cabinets."

"And your painting was hanging just here, you say?" Campbell drew a pointing finger around the shape formed by dust outlines on the wall just above head height.

"You are quite the detective," Mackay said a little sarcastically.

"We were trying to get into this cabinet." Campbell reminded him drily.

Mackay resumed his efforts and with a worrying grating click the drawer unlocked. Mackay lifted out a file tabbed 'Arthur Fraser'. Campbell and Black noticed another file tabbed 'Gordon and Elda Macrae'.

"Did you name this place after your wife, Mr Mackay?" Campbell asked amicably.

"No, it was already named after my wife, sergeant. That had a lot to do with my buying it."

Mackay laid the file on his large desk and opened it with no attempt to conceal its contents from Campbell and Black. He lifted the various pages out and laid them apart like playing cards.

"Nothing much here, gentlemen, I guess you want to check on who this guy is or was? He wasn't a very young man but he seemed a bit young just to be dropping down dead."

"Is that what Mr Macrae told you had happened to him?"

"Well he thought the guy had taken some sort of attack and pulled the bookcase down on top of himself, yeah." Mackay said plainly. "Is that not what happened?"

"It may be what happened. Mr Macrae is describing his first impressions and I am not contradicting him but we must look a little deeper." Campbell explained as Darren Black wrote down details from the paperwork.

"Would it save you chaps time if I just copied all this stuff? Here use this." Mackay offered as he switched on the photocopier. Six pages later they were finished.

"We might need the copier again in a moment, Mr Mackay. What paperwork do you have to describe and confirm the painting?"

Mackay put back the 'Fraser' file and from a lower drawer took out an anonymous file. He withdrew from it his receipt for the Peploe painting. Campbell whistled softly when he saw the price paid to the auction house ten years earlier.

"Thirty-two thousand quid in 1975, what would it fetch now?" Campbell wondered aloud.

"Considerably more." Mackay said confidently. The insurance company are forever revising the value upwards.

Now that it has been stolen they will have to work out the present market price."

"Was the house itself broken into?" Darren Black asked.

"I have seen nothing to suggest that." Mackay said thoughtfully. "I was asking Macrae how anyone could have stolen the painting without breaking in and with him constantly setting the alarm like he says he did."

"Was Mr Macrae coming and going from here? Did he have house keys?" Campbell asked.

"Oh yes, he had keys for the front door and he knows the alarm settings. Any time we are away Gordon takes care of the heating, the aquarium and places any mail in chronological order on the hall table."

"So, you obviously trust him?" Campbell observed.

"I certainly trust Gordon. I just wonder if he has been careless at some time with the alarm or the front door."

Campbell recalled the argument he had heard when he arrived.

"Does his wife play any role in these chores?" Campbell asked.

"Not necessarily but I suppose she might accompany him or help him. I trust her too, actually. I have no reason not to."

"Do you have a photograph of this missing painting, Mr Mackay? It would be helpful to our enquiries to know exactly what the stolen item looks like."

"Yes, I might have a few actually but the best one is attached to the back of the insurance file."

Campbell selected the papers he wanted to copy and was permitted to take the photograph.

"Thank you, Mr Mackay, I understand you are going to Aberdeen tomorrow. Can you give me a number to reach you if any anything develops?"

Mackay pulled out a business card and handed it to Campbell. Darren Black had begun to dust the filing cabinet for fingerprints and lifted those he found. Campbell asked Mackay to provide his own prints for elimination purposes. When this had been done the CID officers prepared to leave.

"My colleague, Andrew Fleming, has the keys of the cottage, Mr Mackay. He locked up after the undertakers had removed the late Mr Fraser. He will retain them until it is possible to return them to you. We would also like to conduct a search of the cottage in line with our enquiries. Have you any objection to our doing so? Ideally you would also be present but I realise that you would be inconvenienced if you need to be in Aberdeen and from what you have said I doubt that you could explain much of anything found."

"I have no objections at all, Sergeant. I have allowed complete strangers to view the property without my being there. You and your colleagues are welcome to search if it helps."

"Thank you again, Mr Mackay. I will be calling on Mr Macrae just as you said."

THREE

As he drove the short distance to the Macrae house, Campbell noticed Darren Black counting something out on his fingers.

"What are you doing?" he asked.

"If the Mackays were married in 1965, their daughter, Lorna, was born three years earlier." Black reasoned.

"Right enough." Campbell agreed. "We will avoid any questions on the matter for the time being, though, ok?"

When they had reached the Macrae cottage, Gordon Macrae opened the front door before they had the opportunity to knock.

"Come in lads." he said in his usual soft lilt, the type of voice most people found pleasant. "My wife has taken to her bed. I told her about how angry Gregor had got over his painting getting stolen and she got quite upset. She is one to get those migraine headaches so she went for a lie down. I'm hoping she is asleep. She is afraid of losing our house over this business."

"Do you think that could happen?" Campbell asked .

"I have never seen the man that angry before." Macrae said. "I don't know what to think."

"According to Mr Mackay his house has not been broken into and he sees that as meaning that it was entered while you had the alarm off. How long did you have the alarm off at a time?"

"Probably no more than an hour at the most. It was usually less." Macrae said softly.

"Were you always alone?" Campbell asked.

"Sometimes Elda was with me but she would stay near the front door. She takes nothing to do with the heating or the aquarium but she knows what to do with the mail."

"Never anyone else?"

"No, nobody else. It's hard to imagine anyone else being around but when I am on my own I leave the front door unlocked while I go to the boiler and the fish tank."

"Where is the boiler?" Campbell asked, wishing he had asked Mackay.

"It is on the ground floor but right at the back of the building beyond the kitchen. The aquarium is in the back sitting room. They call it the garden room because it gives a view over the back gardens."

"Would your wife wait for an hour at the front door for you to come back?" Darren Black asked with obvious disbelief.

"No. I doubt that." Macrae replied with a smile. "If I found things satisfactory I would be back quickly but if there was some resetting or bleeding to be done I would go back and tell her I would be longer at the boiler and she might be better to just go back home."

"So, how do you see this, Mr Macrae? How did this happen? Have you ever forgotten to reset the alarm at any time?" It was Campbell who asked.

"No, never. I can honestly say that I have never left the big house without setting the alarm. I must admit to leaving the front door unlocked while I am there though. I can think of no opportunity for any thief other than that." Macrae said, sounding despondent but truthful.

"Have you kept a note of your visits or was it more a case of the same time each day?" Black asked.

"It was pretty regular, I suppose. I would be there in the morning between eight and nine and in the evening between six and seven. It suited my day best to be going at these times."

"Someone has tried to force open the filing cabinet in the study. What do you know about that?" Campbell asked.

"Nothing." Macrae said immediately with a look of surprise. "Gregor never mentioned it to me."

"No, I don't suppose he would. He didn't know himself at the time he last spoke to you. Someone has tried to force the filing cabinet though, the one beside where the painting hung. Were you ever in that room during your visits?"

"I have been in a couple of times. When the mail builds up on the hall table I take the first of it and put it on his desk but I have no reason to go near the cabinets and I could not be sure about the picture either. I don't bother to put on the light, you see."

"Very well, Mr Macrae. We will go now but we will have to return at some point to speak with Mrs Macrae. I hope she will soon be over her migraine. There is always the possibility that we need to see you again if further questions arise."

As they prepared to leave Campbell turned to Gordon Macrae.

"The death of Arthur Fraser is still being investigated. My colleague Andrew Fleming has the cottage keys and we intend having a better look around the place. You have met him already, I believe."

Macrae nodded.

Gordon Macrae rose early the next morning and left Elda in bed as he made his way to the big house. His wife had stayed in her bed since the CID visit the previous day and had eaten nothing and said only a few words to refuse his offer of food. She had not behaved this way for years. He hoped to put matters right with Gregor Mackay. Elda's concern over their tenancy might be justified.

Gregor Mackay had also risen early and was organising some of the letters received in his absence. He had already notified the insurance company the previous day of the theft of his painting. They had promised a visit from an agent in the next few days. He was therefore happy to receive Gordon Macrae.

Gordon was asked to watch out for the insurance

agent. He also handed Gordon a list of things he wanted attended to before Laura came back from Florida. Gordon accepted the list without complaint. Nothing was said about his tenancy being in jeopardy but Gregor Mackay had maintained a stern countenance while speaking to him. Mackay also expected the holiday chores of watching the heating system and the aquarium to be continued.

Gregor Mackay left for Aberdeen without raising any hint of eviction but his manner suggested that he might still be considering the option. Macrae chose not to mention it either. It just had not seemed an appropriate time. Gordon felt that Mackay was deferring to an appropriate moment for the list of work had not been accompanied by the word 'please'. His hopes would benefit from the return of Laura Mackay.

He looked down at the list and, with Elda still in bed, he felt that he might as well make a start.

Hamish MacLeod had submitted his initial death report to the Procurator Fiscal but had been careful to point out that enquiries were being continued. A post-mortem examination had been ordered and carried out. The pathologist had recorded the cause of death as exsanguination from the head wound which he described as being vertical to the back of the scalp, four inches in length and penetrating the cranium and brain to a depth of 3/4 in. The width of the wound varied between 3/8 and 7/8 in. making it entirely consistent with the head of a poker or similarly shaped metal instrument. Linear bruising over the right templar region was thought to be post-mortem.

Fleming knew that the CID had hoped to close the death of Arthur Fraser as a 'probable accident' in his own home with no other party present or involved. The pathologist had agreed with the Fleming version. Darren Black had told him that Mackay had given consent to the cottage being searched and Fleming wanted to be there but Campbell would probably reject that idea, however, Fleming had the keys. With Hamish MacLeod. He set off for Lauradale.

"What are you hoping to find?" Hamish asked as they drove through a beautiful landscape, transformed overnight by a blanket of snow.

"Anything that helps us identify Arthur Fraser, an address book, letters, receipts or anything at all."

"Somebody somewhere must know this man." Hamish said as he looked out his passenger window. He would never have taken the chance that Fleming was taking but the mischief of the man had always appealed to him.

"Somebody knows him." Fleming said emphatically. "And that somebody hates his guts."

When they reached the cottage Fleming walked around it to ensure that there were no fresh footprints. Once inside, the men noticed just how cold the house was when the fire had not been lit. Fraser would have required to burn his fire in the regular and constant manner described by Gordon Macrae.

Behind the front door there hung a large heavy coat with deep pockets. In one of these pockets Fleming found a small pair of binoculars. The jacket hanging beneath the coat contained three crumpled £1 notes and some change. The drawers mostly contained either unwashed clothing or nothing at all, but one held a notebook, a notepad and several cheap ballpoint pens. Fleming lifted the notebook and flicked through the pages. The early entries were short and consisted of repeated numbers using a nibbed pen and ink. They were randomly spaced with several empty pages between. On one page was written 'L. MACKAY 34 Brechin Way A.' and on another 'M RANKINE 19 GILLESPIE ST F'. Nearer the back of the book was an entry in fresher ink – 'MOTHER BITCH HERE'. Nowhere was there a telephone number or a date.

The writing pad had the beginning of a letter which read, 'Dear Margaret, I know you don't want to hear.' This writing had been scored through as if the author had changed his mind about completing it. Fleming kept both the notebook and notepad.

The body of Arthur Fraser had been removed, the room had been dusted and photographed but the wooden unit still lay on top of spilled books on the floor.

"Give me a hand here, Hamish. Let's get this thing back on its feet." Fleming suggested.

They soon discovered why Campbell and Black had left it alone. The unit was heavier than expected but with extra effort the pair managed to pull it upright. They then began to lift each book in turn and inspect it for any enclosures before placing it back on the unit.

As the floor gradually became clearer of books Fleming noticed a small gold item caught in the shag pile of the large central rug. He picked it out carefully and found it to be a gold teardrop pendant on a fine gold chain. Fleming and MacLeod shuffled the unit back into its exact position against the wall and measured from the base of the unit to the spot where the pendant had lain and then measured from the floor vertically up the front of the unit. It was reasonable to think that the pendant may have lain on the second top shelf of the unit prior to the unit's fall to the floor. The other possibility was that someone had been wearing the pendant and dropped it on top of the rug before the unit came down. Fleming put the pendant and chain in his pocket. Time might tell whose it was and why it should be there.

The pair then went to the bedroom and Fleming removed the photograph from the large frame on the bedside cabinet. The small black and white, somewhat grainy image of a teenage girl also went into Fleming's pocket. He wiped the frame clean. Fleming stuck a hand up the chimney above the clean fireplace of the room and he found that some fabric item was being used to block the chimney. He pulled enough down to see that it was a blue boiler suit but he knew that it would be supporting a load of suit and dirt. He pushed it back again.

The kitchen cupboards showed that Fraser had lived

out of tins, many of which were past their 'sell by' date. Small amounts of leftovers were in plastic food containers with 'snap on' lids.

Now that the books had been replaced, Fleming studied them as a collection. He formed the opinion that they were unlikely to belong to Fraser. They had probably come with the rental of the house and wall unit. They had held no significance for Fraser.

Hamish came from the kitchen carrying a stepladder that he placed beneath the hatch to the attic. He climbed up, pushing the hatch upwards.

"I'm not the first to be up here, Andy. There is a case here and it's not that dirty."

He handed down a smart leather luggage case of medium size with the initials AF on a plastic plate near the handle.

"There's nothing else up here." Hamish declared before closing the hatch and climbing down.

Andrew Fleming laid the case on the table and released the slide catches. As he lifted the lid both men gasped. The contents consisted of money, a lot of money. Bundles of notes in different denominations were held together by rubber bands that had become hard and brittle with age. There were also bank bags filled with coins.

On closer inspection they found that two of the bundles were ten shilling notes and some bags held shillings and half-crowns.

"This lot is pre-decimal." Fleming said quietly, as if to himself. "Where has it been?"

GEORGE MURRAY

"Do you suppose that our Mr Fraser pulled off a bank job in his younger days?" MacLeod suggested with a smirk on his face.

"Looks that way." Fleming agreed. "We'll put it back in the attic, Hamish. Better to give the CID something to find."

Hamish chuckled and shook his head.

Gordon Macrae had spent time at the 'big house' despite knowing full well that the list of jobs could wait. Not only that but they were never his responsibility in the first place. As he set the alarm system and headed for home he wondered if Mackay would seriously consider evicting a seventy year old man and his sixty year old wife from their home. Gregor was a hard-nosed businessman and not the type to enjoy losing a valuable painting but he would surely not become that cruel. What would Laura Mackay say? Gregor's wife was a determined woman who normally settled for nothing less than her own way and evicting old folks from their homes in winter was certainly not her way.

By the time he reached home, Gordon felt easier in his own mind. He hoped that his wife had left her bed by now. He hoped that she was back to her normal self and had cooked dinner. He was hungry but he was to be disappointed. The kitchen showed no hint of cooking or even preparation. His hopes were not to be raised in the lounge either for Elda was not there. From the bedroom upstairs he could hear the slow rambling monotone of

70

Elda talking to herself. Gordon had heard this many times before but not since their move to Lauradale. This was her first drunken soliloquy in years.

He entered the bedroom to find his wife, still in her nightdress, sitting on the edge of their bed with an open bottle of gin in her hand. The gin he knew about, it had been bought when they were still in Glasgow and had remained untouched until now, and now it was almost empty.

Elda did not acknowledge her husband's arrival but continued to babble some incoherent tale, her free hand moved expressively as she spoke. Her focus seemed to be on something leaning against the wall in front of her. Whatever this was, it had not been there this morning. Gordon moved closer. He called out aloud when he recognised the missing painting. His shout had finally brought his wife's babbling to an end.

Gordon picked up the painting and saw that it had been damaged. Just below the centre of the picture there was a one inch tear in the canvas.

"That was me. I did it." Elda said in slurred tones of hopelessness.

"But you stole it, Elda." Gordon said with genuine incredulity. "Why did you steal it?"

"I didn't steal it." she protested, now waving both her hands about. Gordon moved to remove the gin bottle from her grasp and placed it on the window sill.

"I tore it. I just wanted to keep it 'til Laura got home." she explained, her speech slurred and fractured by hiccoughs.

"How did you manage to tear it?" Gordon asked. "You are never near it."

"The knife got jammed in the cabinet. It was stuck real hard and when I pulled at it, the thing came flying back and tore the painting."

"What knife?"

"The big one on Gregor's desk." she said as if Gordon should have known.

"That thing is for opening envelopes, Elda. What were you doing at the filing cabinet anyway?"

"Trying to get in." she said in a voice that suggested the answer was obvious. "I wanted to see what it said in there about that animal over there."

She was waving her hand again, in the general direction of Fraser's cottage.

"Arthur Fraser?" Gordon asked with astonishment. "What do you need to know about Arthur Fraser?"

"How come his name is Arthur Fraser?" she asked, raising a finger as if her question carried an obvious significance. She stretched for the gin bottle but her hand fell well short of reaching it.

"Because that is his name, Elda. The files would tell you that."

"Then the files are lying." she said wearily. She lay back on the bed and closed her eyes.

Gordon placed the painting on top of the wardrobe and replaced the cap on the gin bottle before taking it to the kitchen. Elda had already begun to snore.

In the kitchen he looked at the hand-written list of telephone numbers on a card above the telephone and called Gregor Mackay's Aberdeen office number.

When Fleming arrived for duty the next day he was met by Chief Inspector MacKellar and the Procurator Fiscal.

"Where did you get your registration details for that man Fraser?" the Chief Inspector asked in that superior tone that usually meant trouble.

"From the copy of the extract birth certificate he apparently provided to the letting agency when he secured tenancy of the cottage." Fleming answered, choosing not to point out that the report was Hamish MacLeod's. "I'm sure it said so in the report."

"It turns out that the birth certificate has probably been forged. The same man died in Glasgow in 1982." the Procurator Fiscal explained in a more civilised tone. "His death was the subject of a report to the Glasgow Fiscal. It seems he lived alone in a top floor flat. The man was 70 years of age at the time."

"His cause of death?" Fleming asked.

"He fell down the common staircase. He walked with a stick and it seems he was poor on his feet."

"Do you have the name of the reporting officer, sir?" Fleming asked but the Fiscal was given no chance to answer as MacKellar interrupted.

"What do you want with that Fleming? The CID will deal with this."

"I thought they were tied up in an art theft." Fleming commented.

"The painting has turned up, apparently. Mackay called Detective Sergeant Campbell this morning."

"Then I may expect to hear the true identity of our dead man sometime." the Procurator Fiscal said, reflecting his assessment of CID efforts and the Chief Inspector's gift for rudeness. "Excuse me."

MacKellar stared after him, wondering if the Fiscal had intended any rebuke. Fleming smiled and left MacKellar to stare and wonder.

FOUR

Douglas Campbell called Jack Kelly, the constable who had attended the death of Arthur Fraser in Partick, three years earlier.

According to Kelly, Arthur Fraser had been a widower who resided alone. He had become slow on his feet and walked with a stick. An application had been made for a change of council house to a ground floor flat but then Mr Fraser had not been the only applicant for such a move. He had spent his working life in John Brown's shipyards at Clydebank and had never been in any form of trouble. His wife had predeceased him by eight years and he had no living relatives at the time of his death. His neighbours had known him well over a long number of years and thought it disgraceful that he had not been rehoused.

Despite his slowness on his feet Fraser had never been known to fall. He had met his death by falling down the internal and common stone staircase that served all the flats but no witness had been present to see this. A neighbour had found him and summoned an ambulance but the man was pronounced dead at the scene from a head wound.

Campbell asked Kelly how the man had been identified as Arthur Fraser. He was told that neighbours had quickly gathered around the man when he was found and were still there when the police arrived. They had mostly been neighbours of the man for several years, going back to the time when his wife was alive. They knew he was Arthur Fraser. The council had a long record of his tenancy and his rent payment, something on which he had never defaulted. The mail found in his home was all addressed to him and his GP knew him well.

"So you never came across his birth certificate I suppose?" Campbell asked.

"No, there was nothing like that. There was nothing of any great value in the house either. I had a good look round before the council services came and cleared the place."

"I take it from what you say, that Fraser was not someone with a criminal history?" Campbell suggested.

"Hardly, the old man was never in trouble in his life and nobody saw him as a thief. He had a brother with quite a record but he died a few years back while in prison. Arthur had taken little or nothing to do with him."

"So you have no idea who could be up here with his birth certificate masquerading as him?" Campbell concluded.

"No idea, sorry."

When Detective Sergeant Campbell and Detective Constable Darren Black had conducted their search of the cottage they returned with the leather suitcase full of cash. Campbell was positively elated.

The discovery of a suitcase containing pre-decimal money to the value of nine thousand and sixty-eight pounds and fifteen shillings was circulated as the probable proceeds of crime. Information was requested on any possible outstanding amounts to coincide with this discovery should be forwarded to Corran Bay for the attention of Detective Sergeant Campbell. There were no immediate responses.

Fleming and MacLeod were sitting discussing another matter when Darren Black came into the room and walked up close to Fleming.

"Andy, was it you that removed the picture from the frame in the guy's bedroom? The one of the young girl?"

Fleming looked directly at him.

"Did Campbell send you to ask me, Darren?"

"No," Darren said with a smile. "He never even noticed. If it was you, just tell me that things are okay. If it wasn't you, then we have a mystery."

"We don't have that mystery, Darren." Fleming said frankly.

Darren continued to look at him for a moment, convincing himself that Fleming had the picture.

"All right." the detective said as he turned to leave.

"Darren," Fleming said to his back. "If it ever matters come back to me right?"

"Right Andy."

In the course of other duties Fleming found himself in the vicinity of Lauradale and he wondered if Gregor Mackay had returned from Aberdeen. There was a cottage key to be returned but more importantly, he would like the chance to speak to the man.

He drove to the front of the estate house and saw the pattern of footprints to and from the front door made by Gordon Macrae. On either side of this pattern there was an unbroken carpet of snow that extended around the sides of the big house. At each front corner of the building there stood a large stone cube surmounted by a carved Celtic cross. These looked odd as they gave the impression of a graveyard. Fleming went to the front door and knocked. There was no reply. As he was walking back to his car he thought of the early years of his service and how walking round unlit property at night was greatly helped by the presence of snow. Snow reflected moonlight and without the use of a torch the patrolling officer could see any unexplained footprints.

About to drive away, Fleming became aware of another car driving into the estate behind him. He waited to find that it was the CID car containing Douglas Campbell and Darren Black. Campbell stopped beside Fleming and asked him what brought him there.

"I was just passing the place and I wondered if Mackay was back. We still have his key, remember?"

"We are going up to see Gordon Macrae about the painting. I might just give him the key." Campbell suggested.

"Rather than give it to him, Dougie, why not ask him if he has ever had it before? If not, then perhaps it might be better to wait for Mackay or even the letting agency. Macrae has nothing to do with the Fraser place."

"As you say." Campbell said huffily as he accelerated away.

Back at the police office, Fleming had created two lists, the first of towns beginning with the letter 'A' and headed 34 Brechin Way. The second was of towns beginning with 'F' and the address 19 Gillespie Street. Both addresses taken from the dead man's notebook. He sat by a telephone and a police almanac. One by one he scored off towns that did not have the appropriate addresses. His first success was Aberdeen where he learned that 34 Brechin Way was a bungalow occupied by a Mr and Mrs John Turner. They were in the phone book but when Fleming tried the number he got no reply. 'Probably both at work' he thought.

Now he turned his attention to the towns beginning with 'F' and having a 19 Gillespie Street. Influenced by the previous address in Aberdeen he enquired with the police at Fortrose, Fraserburgh, Forfar and Forres before Darren Black entered the room and interrupted him.

"Did you get the painting?" Fleming asked expectantly.

"Yeah. It's in the CID room." Black replied with enthusiasm. "It's damaged. There's a hole in it."

"Was it like that when Macrae found it?" Fleming asked.

"Yes. So he says."

"When and where is he saying he found it?" Fleming pressed.

"Yesterday afternoon. He says he found it behind one of the Celtic crosses at the end of the big house."

"Was it inside a bag or something?" Fleming asked. "It's not exactly ideal weather for a painting to be outside."

"When he gave it to us the painting was in a plastic bag but not the one he had found it in. According to him the original bag had been filthy and wet, so he had put it out."

"So he is saying that he found the painting yesterday behind one of the big Celtic crosses at the front of the big house?" Fleming asked slowly and deliberately.

"Yeah." Black confirmed.

"I take it Dougie never went to the spot where it was allegedly found?"

"No. You can see it from the road." young Black said easily.

"Aye, I know Darren. We were all there earlier today, remember? The snow that covers the garden fell overnight on Monday into Tuesday. It has stayed unbroken since. There are no footprints anywhere near either of the crosses and the same snow would have covered the bag containing the bag with the painting. So how has Macrae managed to recover that painting from a place that no-one had visited since the snow fell?"

Darren Black looked stunned.

"We never thought of checking on that." he said

almost apologetically. "Dougie saw no reason to disbelieve Macrae. He has every right to walk round the big house and he seems like such an honest old bloke."

"Yes." Fleming agreed. "I thought so too, Darren, but even honest men make footprints in the snow."

"Thanks Andy." Darren said as he turned to leave.

Fleming went back to his list and called Central Scotland Police at Falkirk. The voters roll showed that Mrs Margaret Rankine resided at 19 Gillespie Street. Fleming was given her telephone number from the phone book.

His call was eventually answered by a quietly spoken, elderly lady. She confirmed to Fleming that she was Mrs Margaret Rankine and he explained who he was.

"I have been dealing with the death of a man who lived alone and was not particularly well known to many people. Those who had some contact with him thought his name was Fraser, but that may not be the case. One piece of information available to me is an entry in the man's notebook. The entry might refer to yourself as it contains 19 Gillespie Street followed by the letter 'F'. This could mean Falkirk or any town beginning with 'F'. There are very few entries in his book so this person obviously meant something to this man. Have you any suggestions?"

For a few seconds nothing was said but the old lady was still on the phone, making quiet noises that Fleming could not interpret.

"It could be George." she said quietly and a little reluctantly.

"George being?" Fleming asked, purposefully lowering his own voice.

"George is my brother, Officer Fleming. I last saw him about three years ago when he came out of prison. He wanted to stay with me but my husband was still alive at that time and . . . it was just out of the question."

"What is George's surname, Mrs Rankine?"

"Prentice. He is George Prentice."

Fleming was then informed of the reasons for George Prentice's incarceration. He noted the tone of Mrs Rankine's account and judged that she had seen her brother as guilty of the crimes with which he had been convicted. He also noted from her, George Prentice's date of birth, his former employment and his former address.

"Did your brother give you any idea of his plans after he left you, Mrs Rankine?"

"He asked me if I knew where the Turnbulls had moved to. Laura Turnbull had been his girlfriend when they were teenagers together but her parents moved away and that split George and Laura up. There were rumours after Laura left that she had been pregnant but that wasn't necessarily true, it certainly wasn't why they moved. Mr Turnbull had got a job with an oil company. I told George that they had probably gone to Aberdeen or even Shetland but I really had no idea."

"Did you give him any money?" Fleming asked.

"No, I don't remember him asking for any. Do they give men money when they come out of prison?"

"I have no idea, Mrs Rankine, sorry. If they do I wouldn't expect it would be much. Did you give him anything, other than money?"

"Well yes. I had taken some of his things from Mum's house when George went into prison. Mum was dead but I could only take smaller items that he asked me to keep for him. I gave him an old photograph of Laura Turnbull. It was small and a bit shabby but it seemed to still mean something to him." she said with her first indicative tones of sympathy.

"Did George have a suitcase with him when he visited you?" Fleming asked without inference.

"Yes, he did. He said he had 'picked up' that nice suitcase. It was smaller than usual but real leather and quite smart. He never said exactly where he had picked it up."

"Thank you Mrs Rankine. I suspect from what you tell me, that your brother could well be the man who has died here but I have further enquiry to make and will get back to you."

"Should I tell Mr Scott about this?" the old lady asked.

"Who is Mr Scott?"

"Some kind of probation officer, I think. He came here after George got out of prison. I had been down as the next of kin apparently and Mr Scott thought he might be with me. I told him that George had been here but had gone and I did not expect him to come back. He asked me to call him if I heard from George. I still have his card somewhere."

"If you still have his number then call him." Fleming advised. "Don't give him any information just ask him to call me."

Replies began to come into the office in response to the circulation of the suitcase and its old money contents. Most were vague or improbable but one report caught the eye.

In December 1967 a large department store in Glasgow had its safe blown open by an experienced safecracker called Thomas Fraser. Fraser had served time for his crime and then died in prison in 1982. The total cash stolen from the safe amounted to £12,322 and it had never been recovered.

"That must be the brother of Arthur Fraser, the brother that Kelly spoke about." Campbell told Darren Black. "But I am not sure that it helps us. Thomas Fraser was a loner by all accounts, even where his brother was concerned and the brother took little to do with him. He never worked with an accomplice and hardly spoke to other cons about his work. He had told the police and the court that the money was lost. According to this telex massage he had left the money in a skip full of waste only to return to an empty skip." Campbell shrugged his shoulders. "Even if it is the same money, just about anybody could have come across it."

"Was it in his brother's suitcase when he dumped it?" Black asked sceptically.

Campbell drew him a look that suggested the Detective Sergeant preferred his own unconsidered version.

Darren Black later related the conversation to Fleming.

"Who was the cop that Campbell spoke to at Partick, the one that handled the brother's death?" Fleming asked.

"Kelly, Jack Kelly."

It was into the evening before Fleming got a response on the Aberdeen number. His call was answered by John D. Turner, an American gentleman. Fleming explained who he was and that he was trying to establish the identity of a man who died.

"If the letter A stands for Aberdeen Mr Turner, then your address may have some connection to the name Mackay." Fleming told him.

"Yeah, well you could be on the right trail there, Officer Fleming. I bought this house from a guy Mackay, another oilman from Texas. I don't recall his first name but the man had a wife and daughter."

"Where was he moving to, Mr Turner? Did he tell you that?"

"Nope, sorry. Place names don't mean much to me even now but back then I had no idea where anywhere was in Scotland. It was over to the west of the country, I know that."

"And this move was when exactly?" Fleming asked.

"We moved in here in '75." Turner said slowly. "Just been saying how we been livin' here for ten years, just like the Mackays did. So he told me."

"Has anyone else enquired with you about a Laura Mackay or a Laura Turnbull?" Fleming asked.

"Nope. Who is Laura Turnbull?"

"Same person. Mrs Mackay's maiden name would have been Turnbull."

"Oh, I see. No, I don't recall anyone asking after these folks. Can I get your number so I can call you if I hear anything or remember anything that might matter?"

Fleming left the office number with Turner.

As he put the phone down Fleming wondered how George Prentice, for that was indeed his deceased's name, had been able to trace Laura Turnbull to her married name and address in Aberdeen. Prentice would have done a similar exercise to the one Fleming had just done, but with a telephone directory. How many Turnbulls would there be in Aberdeen? The guy had been persistent. The Turnbulls had moved over twenty years ago, would they still be in Aberdeen? Gregor Mackay would know, if all suppositions were correct, he was related by marriage.

Fleming managed to contact Jack Kelly the following morning. He acknowledged that the CID had already pursued the matter with Kelly but Fleming was after more detail with a view to tracing the connection to the recently deceased man. He asked Kelly to describe everything he found as he attended Arthur Fraser's death. Was the door locked or unlocked? Was the old man dressed to be going somewhere outside the building when he fell down the stairs? What was his house like inside? Did he smoke?

Kelly remembered that the house door had been locked.

The old man had been wearing his coat and cap. The house key had been in his coat pocket. The flat was clean and tidy, especially so for an old man living alone. There was nothing to say that he had smoked. He was dressed for going out and might have been going to buy more screws.

"How do you know that?" an intrigued Fleming asked.

"He had taken the front panel off his bath. It couldn't have been easy for that thing had been painted over a hundred times." Kelly said this as if he felt the old man's frustration. "Old Arthur would want new screws for putting it back on."

"Was there anything under the bath to explain why he had done this?" Fleming asked. "Had there been a leak?"

"Nothing but dust and some old sawdust. There was no sign of a leak. I hate to think how long that bath had been boxed in." Kelly said, missing the point completely.

"Did you notice a suitcase in the flat?" Fleming asked. "A suitcase with the initials AF on it?"

"No, I never saw it if it was there. I dare say I could have missed seeing something like that if it wasn't in plain sight."

"Right, Jack." Fleming agreed. "Oh, before I forget, was Tom Fraser the safe-blower a brother to Arthur Fraser?"

"Funny you should ask that." Jack Kelly said with enthusiasm. "I never mentioned it to your mate, Campbell, because I didn't know this at the time. I was talking to some of the boys about Campbell's phone call and Arthur Fraser. One of the guys here has been here for years. He told me that Tommy Fraser was actually caught running out of his brother's flat on the night of the big January storm in 1968. That was when he got caught for the job that put him inside."

So the brothers were close at that time." Fleming suggested.

"Well they must have been but according to Arthur's neighbours, Arthur never went once to visit his brother in prison. Tom Fraser had died in prison and Arthur had said that he regretted never having visited his brother."

"Did they say if anyone ever visited Arthur?" Fleming enquired.

"No. Arthur went out to the shops and stopped at the pub for a pint on the way back, apparently, but he was never out at night and nobody ever knocked his doors except the neighbours."

"Okay, Jack, thanks. I get the picture."

Fleming did have a picture, but an unsubstantiated picture of someone visiting Arthur Fraser and encouraging him to remove his bath panel, or allowing his visitor to remove it to obtain the hidden money. With the money removed to his suitcase, Arthur had been encouraged to take the money to the police and explain where it had come from. In trusting his visitor he had left the house, only to be thrown down his stairs and left there without his suitcase.

Arthur Fraser was an honest old man. If he had known the secret location of the money would he have taken two years to retrieve it? For the person who did know why had it taken them two years to visit Arthur Fraser?

Fleming remembered his conversation with Margaret Rankine and what she had said about her brother having a suitcase with him when he visited in 1982, a suitcase that he had 'picked up'. Fleming also recalled the Barlinnie dowts in the dead man's ashtray. The real Arthur Fraser did not smoke and had certainly never been to prison.

Douglas Fraser had taken the fingerprints of the dead man but had no name for comparison purposes other than 'Arthur Fraser', a man with no criminal record at all. Fleming told Campbell of his conversation with Margaret Rankine and how he believed that a comparison with the prints of George Prentice might provide a hit. Campbell had submitted his forms for comparison, asking that the matter receive urgent attention as the subject had now been dead for over a week. Fleming noticed how it cheered Campbell to learn that the deceased man had a sister. She could attend to funeral matters once the body was cleared by the Fiscal.

Andrew Fleming was confident that the fingerprints would match and show the deceased to be George Prentice. That would resolve the matter of identity but not the matter of motive. Dougie Campbell would relax a little to know that his murder victim was a convicted murderer and rapist who was a loss to nobody, not even the man's sister. Who would mourn the passing of such a man?

If, as the pathologist had observed, Prentice had been killed by a blow from the poker, it was still not clear who would have cause to have dealt the blow. It was so much easier to go with the bizarre accident theory involving a heavy wooden unit pulled down by the man himself. If that was to be the police deduction then who would argue? Fleming could almost hear the wheels turning in Campbell's head.

Fleming could all but hear the conversation between Campbell and MacKellar as they tried to convince each other that the accidental death would answer all the questions, tick all the boxes. Who would criticise the results of enquiry when nobody particularly cared for the victim? They could not see how there would be any grieving party for George Prentice. Fleming was not sure about that and he was absolutely sure that they were wrong to settle for anything but the absolute truth.

There was still this business of the painting. That had always been a CID affair and the heat was off a bit now that it had been recovered but just like the murder of George Prentice there was no satisfactory ending, only a recovered painting.

Fleming lifted the phone and called the Eastern Division, Glasgow, asking to be connected to Detective Superintendent Johnston. Jimmy Johnston and Fleming had played football together in their younger days, to say nothing of nights at the Electric Garden, the Plaza at Eglinton Toll and other venues.

Several minutes were spent in pleasant re-acquaintance before Johnston asked what he could do for his old pal. Fleming made his account of the circumstances as brief as he could before asking the Detective Superintendent if he knew who had handled the murder for which Prentice had been convicted.

"That was a bit before our time, Andy, but from memory, it was old Jock Cameron. I was at his retirement 'do' and that case seemed to be a bit of a highlight for old Jock. I'll check that I'm right first, but I assume you want to speak to him, right?"

"I do, if he has no objections." Fleming answered.

"You'll be lucky to get him to shut up, Andy. These old guys like to reminisce and old Jock is no exception. I'll get back to you."

Dougie Campbell had decided not to give the cottage key to Gordon Macrae and because Fleming had been the one to put him off doing so, he had given the key back to Fleming for him to return. It was still in Andrew Fleming's pocket. For some reason he felt reluctant to return it just yet. Since searching the cottage with Hamish MacLeod, he had heard from Darren Black of the conversation between Campbell and Mackay. Prentice had wanted to install a central heating system in the cottage. That was hardly surprising for the place was an ice-box, particularly the bedroom. He recalled the clean hearth and the boiler suit stuck up the chimney. He had not seen a need to search that boiler suit. Why had Prentice never lit a fire in that room? Time was running out for Fleming to address this question. He made a point of having Hamish with him as he returned. It had to be done now. The case would stop with the return of the fingerprint analysis.

Torch in hand, Fleming went directly to the bedroom and looked up the chimney. The boiler suit was rolled up and stuffed well above the drawplate. He pulled it down by using the tongs from the main fireplace in the front room. As expected the boiler suit brought with it a lot of soot and dirt. He unrolled the garment and searched the pockets. In the first top pocket he searched, he found a small envelope addressed to Arthur Fraser at his Partick address. The letter read, 'Dear brother Arthur, If you are reading this then I am dead. I want you to know you are lying on a fortune every Friday and Monday, Your loving brother, Tom'.

"What the hell does that mean?" Hamish asked.

"I think George Prentice probably asked the same question, Hamish. He might even have waited two years for his answer. I am guessing that Arthur took a bath every Friday and Monday night."

Fleming returned the cottage key to the letting agents, having found nothing else of interest. He asked if anyone had enquired there recently about the estate cottage or the man living there.

"There was a Probation Officer just before Christmas."

the girl said. "But he was interested in a different man, not Arthur Fraser."

"What name was he looking for?" Fleming asked.

"I don't remember." the girl replied honestly.

Fleming took the boiler suit and letter to Douglas Campbell.

"Great," said Campbell. "The records office called this morning to confirm that our man was George Prentice. He came out of prison and robbed Arthur Fraser of his brother's money. That explains everything."

"Everything except who killed Prentice." Fleming said flatly.

Campbell drew him a dark look as he left the room. Fleming looked across at Darren Black who had been silently watching and listening.

"No prizes for guessing where he's going." Fleming said with disgust.

"No prizes for guessing the outcome either," said Darren. "Murder, what murder?"

About half an hour later, when Fleming was checking a report on another matter, Chief Inspector MacKellar came into the room.

"Detective Sergeant Campbell has told me about the boiler suit and the letter. These items show the connection between Prentice and Fraser's stolen money. Douglas Campbell has explained it to me."

"Yes sir, after I explained it to him." Fleming said abruptly.

"Well anyway, I can see no reason to keep calling this death a murder now. It would be a waste of time and serve no interest at all." He stopped, expecting some sort of outburst from Fleming but when none was forthcoming he continued. "So you will submit a further report to the effect that there are no suspicious circumstances. You can always claim credit for finding the boiler suit and the letter."

Now Fleming reacted.

"If I am submitting any report, Chief Inspector, I will decide what it says. You do expect me to sign my report, don't you?"

MacKellar stared back. This was the Fleming he recognised.

"Yes, I expect you to sign it, but then I have to sign it too, so remember that when you write it." The Chief Inspector said in a cold menacing way, before turning to the door and leaving the room. As he left Hamish entered.

"What's wrong with him?" Hamish asked.

"He is the north end of a southbound horse, Hamish," Fleming said calmly. "Other than that he is all right."

Macleod laughed out loud, just as the phone began to ring. Fleming lifted it to find that he had Detective Superintendent Johnston on the line.

"Andy, I was right. It was Jock Cameron that dealt with the murder and rape of the wee lassie that put Prentice inside. I spoke to him and he would be delighted to discuss it with you. I have his phone number and address for you. He stays in Bearsden."

Fleming noted the details.

"Thanks J.J., you're a pal." Fleming said cheerily.

"I know Andy - and that thought still gives me sleepless nights. Are the CID not dealing with this case?"

"Yes, of course they are Jim, but dealing with it and solving it are two different things."

"I hear you, Andy. Not my area, what can I say? Enjoy yourself with Jock. Glad I could help."

Fleming felt better now. When he had finished what he was doing he would write a supplementary report on the death of George Prentice, explaining how it had become a matter for the CID. Following their enquiry they adjudged there to be no suspicious circumstances. MacKellar could not argue with that. The Procurator Fiscal had been standing beside him when MacKellar had decreed that the CID would enquire into the death of the (then) unknown deceased.

FIVE

Chief Inspector MacKellar was quietly fuming as he read the careful wording of Fleming's report but he signed it and tossed it into his 'out' tray to go to the Procurator Fiscal. The next item in his 'in' tray was a request for him to assign a suitably qualified officer to attend a week-long training course in Glasgow on the subject of Crime Prevention.

A cruel smile spread across his face.

"I have the very man." he said smugly to himself.

In the Macrae household the lack of further visits from the CID had unsettled Elda Macrae. The atmosphere was still tense with nothing much being said between Gordon and his wife. She had stopped drinking again, certainly, but she was still too much like the Elda of old, the woman she had been before they were married, a woman on edge. Gordon had no wish to see a return to these days.

"Elda, I am sick of this silence." he told her earnestly. "Whatever it is that's eating at you is something we need to talk about, so let's talk about it."

"There's nothing to talk about, Gordon. Things are

bad enough without talking about them. Maybe when Laura Mackay comes home we will know if we are staying or being thrown out."

"Laura Mackay would never throw us out, Elda. She's not the type to do that." Gordon reasoned. "That painting meant more to Gregor than it did to Laura. Anyway, nobody else knows that you took it. I lied to protect you, Elda and you know I hate lying. Now you won't even speak to me."

Elda looked at him without speaking. She knew how honest and good he was and how much his lying would have damaged him. It just was not in his true nature.

"I am sorry, Gordon, I really am. I had thought of telling Laura the truth. She would understand better than Gregor."

"She wouldn't understand you trying to get into that filing cabinet, Elda." Gordon pointed out.

"I think she would." Elda said coldly, as if distracted. "But I won't mention that bit. I'll tell her I was taking the picture down to admire it and let it slip against the corner of the cabinet. You see, Gordon, I could always lie better that you."

"That's nothing to be proud of, Elda." Gordon said with a shake of his head. "You are my wife and I have no way of knowing if you have been completely honest with me."

"I haven't told you any lies, Gordon, but there are things I just don't talk about. That's not telling lies."

"Like Laura, your own Laura?" he asked quietly.

His wife span her head towards him and drew a sharp intake of breath.

"You know about Laura?" she asked with obvious alarm and disappointment.

"Did you really think that I could be staying in your house for all these years without learning about Laura?" Gordon replied in his usual soft tones. "You don't remember the early days like I do, Elda. You never knew what you were saying half the time."

"I never told you about Laura." Elda said with feeling.

"No, at least not the whole story, you didn't. There were people around us in Glasgow who just assumed that I would know and they would speak about Laura's murder until they realised that I hadn't actually known what they were talking about."

Elda Macrae was looking down at the floor, more despondent than ever.

"I never wanted you to know, Gordon. I never wanted to be speaking about it ever again to anyone. I still don't."

"Then we won't talk about it, Elda, but knowing about it helped me to understand you better. Bottled-up secrets could never do you any good and never do the two of us any good."

His wife made no reply. She continued to stare down at the carpet. He went to the kitchen and made tea. When he returned, a few minutes later with two mugs of tea, he asked his wife, "Elda, if that was not Arthur Fraser in that cottage then who was it?"

"I don't know, Gordon." she said, a little too positively. "I never said he was somebody else but he acted weird when we saw him at New Year. That was the first time that I saw him up close and he looked really nervous."

"I thought the chap was just shy, Elda, like someone who had spent too much time on his own, maybe." Gordon said sympathetically.

"No, Gordon, that wasn't shy, that was guilty." Elda said with feeling.

"Guilty of what?" Gordon asked.

"That's what I hoped to find in that filing cabinet." Elda said, sipping her tea and looking thoughtful. "But I never got it open."

If it had amused MacKellar to put Fleming down for a week's training in Glasgow then Fleming himself was less than amused. It would mean a week away from his wife and family, sleeping in a training centre or rented room with no company in the evening. He had been on these courses before and knew what a boring time he could expect. On this occasion, however, there just might be a silver lining. He lifted the telephone and dialled the number James Johnston had given him.

"Mr Cameron, Mr Jock Cameron? This is Andrew Fleming."

"That is not such a great amount of damage." the insurance assessor observed as moved about in front of the Peploe painting, adjusting his camera and taking a series of shots. "I see no reason why this painting could not be restored successfully and the sooner, the better."

"Well, it is the subject of a theft enquiry, Mr Hartwell. The enquiry is still open and while we are investigating the theft it must remain as it is and in our possession." Douglas Campbell explained.

"It was found outside the owner's house and nothing else was stolen from Mr Mackay's house, I understand. That does not sound to me like any other art theft, sergeant."

"No." Campbell agreed. "We could expect the painting to be miles away by now, damaged or not."

"Quite so and probably not damaged at all. Art thieves are not that stupid, Sergeant Campbell. I will speak to Mr Mackay and see how he wishes to proceed." Hartwell said while he packed his camera into its bag. "In the meantime, I will take my photographs to an authority on Peploe and seek an auction house valuation. With that I can obtain an estimation for repair and restoration. Thank you for your time, Sergeant Campbell."

Douglas Campbell walked the insurance assessor to his car and watched him drive away. He thought about the observation that this did not look like a normal art theft. Darren Black had already told Campbell of Fleming's comments regarding the improbability of the painting having been retrieved from behind either of the Celtic crosses without the creation of footprints in the snow. He still had to interview Mrs Macrae, Campbell reminded himself.

He returned to his office and spent time carefully wrapping the painting in bubble wrap and brown paper. Then he waited for Darren Black to return from his present enquiry. He was still waiting an hour later when the telephone rang and he answered it to find Gregor Mackay on the line.

"Sergeant Campbell, I have been speaking to the insurance company in the form of Derek Hartwell. I understand he has been to see you and has also seen the painting. He apparently has serious reservations about the theft of the painting but no such doubts about the damage. It seems that the insurance cover would apply equally to the damage and would permit restoration of the painting to its original condition. That could prove lengthy and costly but I would still have ownership of a Peploe when it was finished. I am happy to accept the return of the painting by the police to allow the restoration to begin. If that makes prosecution of any thief more difficult, then too bad. I can gain nothing from a prosecution. I can gain a lot more from restoration and this man recommends that we start that process as soon as possible."

"Why?" Campbell gasped.

"I want that painting restored or at least in the process of being restored when my wife comes home next month. I can always tell her that I have sent it for cleaning or something of that sort. That way she has no worry about thieves visiting her home."

"So, you are prepared to drop your complaint of theft?" Campbell asked, wondering how he could now doctor the figures that looked like flattering his annual performance.

"If that is what it takes to release the painting to the restorers, yes." Mackay said positively. "In the interests of peace and harmony, I consider that best. I will tell the Macraes not to breathe a word of the theft to my wife and daughter. If you require some written disclaimer then let me know and but I want this business out of circulation by the time my family come home."

"All right, Mr Mackay, I'll discuss this development with my superiors and get back to you." Campbell said, scarcely disguising his disappointment. He had little chance of ever detecting an art thief but the statistical value of property stolen against the value of property recovered would have provided impressive reading. Misleading perhaps, but then people who read statistics are ready to be misled.

He thought about his planned interview with Mrs Elda Macrae but with the theft case aborted and the death of George Prentice heading for a 'No action' disposal from the Procurator Fiscal, there seemed to be little point in speaking to her at all. He would speak to MacKellar instead and then to Detective Chief Inspector Adams, his distant CID boss, some eighty miles away. MacKellar and Campbell easily reached a decision to terminate enquiry at Lauradale as having no viability.

They would contact Raymond Adam and put their joint opinions to him.

Adam was not a man to be readily convinced. He knew his callers too well.

"I noticed that you have cancelled your circulation of the stolen painting." Adam said slowly, "- 'recovered at the home of the owner in circumstances not amounting to theft'. It would appear that you are not anxious to work on what exactly happened here. What about the death of that chap on the same estate?"

"It is much the same thing." MacKellar said assertively. "Death was due to a blow on the head but then a heavy item of furniture had fallen on top of him."

"Were you at the cottage to see this for yourself?" Adam asked.

"Well, no actually. I am told by Douglas Campbell what he found. He is here with me. There was nothing to say that there was anyone else present when this happened."

"You have the follow-up death report?"

"Yes."

"Send me a copy."

MacKellar was less confident now. Raymond Adam had already put down his phone.

The Crime Prevention course was proving to be more interesting than Fleming expected. Representatives of leading manufacturers of security technology were present to describe the services available and the advances being made.

Alarm companies had received harsh criticism for the high incidence of FAGI calls (false alarm with good intent) which had meant that 97% of calls received for police attention were of no criminal significance. There had been a great deal of pressure exerted on the alarm companies to improve the performance of their product.

Interesting or not, the course was not uppermost in Fleming's mind. Wednesday evening was the agreed time for him to visit the Bearsden home of Jock Cameron.

Like most addresses in the area, the Camerons' home was a neat old bungalow which Fleming found without difficulty. Jock and his wife Margaret were warm in their welcome. They took an interest in Andy's home life and family, appreciating the scenic environment of where he lived.

Eventually, with Margaret Cameron off to the kitchen, Jock Cameron pointed to a cardboard folder on the coffee table.

"In there are all the newspaper photos and stories collected from the Laura Purdie murder, Andrew. You can take them away to read, but I want them back."

Fleming lifted the folder and opened it to see the extent of the contents. They were original cuttings from different newspapers with nothing to hold them together except the folder itself.

"Thanks Mr Cameron, I will read them and bring them

back to you on Friday. What I really want from you is your memory of the case and the people involved. What happened as far as the police knew? Any aspects of the case that I won't find in the newspapers, that's what I need."

Jock Cameron was nodding his head.

"George Prentice has served time and been released." Fleming said. "For whatever reason, he chooses to live alone, like a hermit, in a wooded estate, avoiding any official scrutiny or suspicion by taking the identity of a dead convict's late brother." Fleming explained the Fraser connection he had learned from Jack Kelly.

"It sounds as if he could have done better for himself." Cameron remarked. "He was a first class heating engineer, you know."

"Well, that explains something to me right away." Fleming said with a smile. "But why go to a cold, damp cottage on a highland estate where he was being refused permission to install heating. He could just as easily have gone to somewhere warm and comfortable? What was his motive for staying and what motive would someone have nowadays to be killing him?"

"He was murdered?" Cameron exclaimed. "If he was murdered then why are the CID not dealing with it?"

Fleming described the scene at the cottage the day the death was reported. He told Cameron of the poker stuck in the ashes; the indentation in the wall; the wound on Prentice's head and the heavy unit that had fallen on top of Prentice's body. He described how the edge of the unit was free from blood and not consistent with the head wound in the way that the poker head was. The CID were involved and they had the same facts that Fleming had just related.

Jock Cameron was quiet and thoughtful for a few moments.

"He was on this estate for the past two years, you say. Had he made any enemies there?"

"No sir, I don't think he was actually known to any of them, except as Arthur Fraser. There seemed to be little contact between Prentice and any of the other people on the estate."

"So, you wonder about motive and think it might be found in their past life? Prentice raped and strangled a fifteen years old girl that he had only just met. I wondered about his motive back then. He had already given plenty of folks a reason to hate him. I tried to get him to explain himself and tell me exactly what had happened but he never did say. He never admitted to killing the girl but he never denied it either, not in any specific way. He would just say, 'I would never hurt my Laura', almost as if he was trying to convince himself. This was a twenty-three year old man talking about a fifteen year old girl he had only just met. I wondered about his mental state but the doctor reckoned he was sane enough, just in a state of denial. He had got rough and violent in seeking to have sex and may well have strangled the girl as part of his physical control to keep her resistance to a minimum. If this was the case, the doctor had reasoned, he may not have intended to strangle her to death."

"Was there evidence of resisting?" Fleming asked.

"There was heavy bruising over her abdomen and lower chest and clear signs of manual strangulation round her throat. The police surgeon found scratch marks around that area too and fingernail impressions around her neck, deep impressions. I remember telling him later that Prentice did not have long fingernails, quite the opposite, his nails were bitten down to the quick. The tips of his fingers had grown over the top of his nails. That takes a lifetime of nail-biting. He could not possibly have left fingernail impressions. The surgeon's response was that the girl herself could have made the impressions in seeking desperately to prise his fingers away from her neck. Nowadays with all this forensic mumbo-jumbo we would have a more certain view of that, but back in the day," he shrugged. "We went with what the police surgeon said. It was '63 after all."

"Prentice had only just met the girl?" Fleming questioned.

"According to the show folks at the 'Waltzer' they met up there and walked away together. Prentice's mother told me that he had no regular girlfriends and spent most of his time either at home or at a football match. The girl's mother described her daughter as a tearaway who would brag about her boyfriends just to annoy her mother but there had never been any mention of a George Prentice. Her boyfriends were usually younger guys."

"She could have been his wee sister." Fleming observed.

"Aye, age-wise, you're right but there was no evidence of any relationship between them. The girl's mother had never heard of a George Prentice as I say and there was no suggestion from the girl's acquaintances that she had known him prior to that day."

"With that level of unfamiliarity, what was all this 'couldn't hurt my Laura' business?" Fleming asked. "Why would he be referring to her that way?"

"I've no idea." Cameron answered. "I asked him that very question several times. He wouldn't give an explanation beyond repeating what he had said, as if the girl was sacred to him. Everyone should just accept that he would never hurt her."

"Not much of a defence then." Fleming said. "But what about the prosecution case, what pointed the finger at Prentice?"

"We recovered his cigarette lighter on the ground not far from the body. It was engraved with the initials G.P. and it had his fingerprints on it. On his trousers there were semen stains either side of the zip and dirt staining on the knees of his trousers from the soft ground beneath the leaves where the girl was found. There were bits of dried leaves in the turn-ups of his trousers and inside his shoes. A young lad had seen him staggering out of the woods as if he had been running a distance and was out of breath.

The boy noticed that Prentice had dirty knees and was muttering to himself, although the boy had no idea what was being said. Just after he had he had seen Prentice, the boy says he heard a loud scream from within the woods. Prentice starting running again and the wee boy took off as well. He certainly wasn't for going in to investigate." Jock said, smiling to himself at the memory of the boy.

"So who had screamed?" Fleming asked.

Cameron shrugged his shoulders.

"We never found that out. Someone may well have come across the body and screamed. If the person concerned did not report it right away, and nobody did, then they probably thought it better not to report it at all. Even the young boy did not come forward until three days into the enquiry."

"So, how did you find Prentice?" Fleming asked.

"One of the fathers at the fairground with his child had seen him walking with the girl. The witness worked at the swimming pool and he recognised Prentice as the guy who usually worked on their heating boiler at the pool. When Laura Purdie's picture appeared in the paper the witness came forward. He also recognised the girl he had seen with Prentice from the photo in the paper. It turned out that several people had seen the couple walking together round the fairground and they were seen leaving together in the direction of these woods."

"Prentice never admitted to any of this?" Fleming asked.

"He never said anything. Like the doctor said, he was in a state of denial. In the end I think that worked against him. The jury probably wondered, like the rest of us, why an innocent man would have absolutely nothing to say" Cameron supposed.

"Was there anything about the case that bothered you, Mr Cameron? Anything that just didn't sit right, if you know what I mean?"

"I suppose the girl's mother bothered me." Cameron remembered. "I think she told the truth but her demeanour was not what I would have expected from a mother who had just lost her only child. The mother was not married, nor had she been, so there was no father to be notified. She did not know who he was apparently."

"What was strange about the mother?"

"There just seemed to be more regret than grief, Andrew. She was angry at everyone, coming up with excuses for her daughter being in a position to be killed. It didn't seem natural. Other people felt a specific hatred against Prentice but she was not spiteful towards Prentice personally. I just found her quite different from your typical Glasgow bereaved parent. Then there was the young boy who saw Prentice coming out of the woods. He was from Easterhouse on the other side of Glasgow and had dogged off school for the day. He had just jumped onto a bus and gone across town for no particular reason. He had no sense of where he actually was. He had been at the fairground but after that he was just lost."

"… and it took him three days to come forward?"

"Yes, again it was the press coverage that made him realise that he might have seen the girl's killer. His folks made him speak up. Cameron recalled, his eyes fixed on the cardboard folder.

"Are you in any doubt about the guilt of Prentice?" Fleming asked firmly.

"No, Andrew, I have always believed Prentice to be the guilty man. I just feel sorry that I could not pick up on what the guy was all about. He was a strange chap, so quiet, so introverted. He gave me no inkling on his side of the story. I wondered if he really had it in him to kill someone intentionally. He had no criminal history to suggest that he could kill, but now, with this Arthur Fraser business, I suppose he could be a killer when it suits him right enough."

"Yes, but Arthur Fraser has not left anyone who might want revenge." Fleming pointed out. "So, Prentice's only known crime that stands to be avenged is the death of Laura Purdie. You said her mother described her as a tearaway, how much did she mean by that" Fleming asked, recalling how Cameron had said the mother blamed her daughter.

"Oh, I think she meant that the girl was promiscuous for her age, Andrew. The mother obviously knew more than we did and found her daughter's attitude hard to take. The way the girl dressed was provocative for the time, mini skirt, lipstick and padded bra. She was trying to look older than she really was and there are few reasons for a girl doing that."

"She had cigarettes and money?" Fleming asked.

"Not that I know of but the witnesses at the fairground say that she had cigarettes and money. Her pal, the girl she had gone there with, said she had a pound note and change, stolen from her mother's purse. She had nothing on her when we found her. Prentice could have taken them and of course, he was saying nothing about anything."

"Yet he left his own cigarette lighter behind?" Fleming remarked. "What about this friend who was with her before Prentice, what part did she play?"

"None really. The girl had met Laura as arranged and they had walked round together for a while until the other girl stopped to speak to somebody she knew and when she ran to catch up with Laura she couldn't find her. She had no idea that Laura was missing until Laura's mother came to her house the next day, looking for Laura. That was when the girl was reported as missing."

"Can you remember the pal's name, Mr Cameron?"

"Not off the top of my head, but I dare say her name and the name of the young man I mentioned might be in these press cuttings. The papers covered the trial. I have no idea where you could find them now."

"No, I dare say." Fleming replied, making his host laugh.

After sharing tea and scones with the Camerons, Fleming returned to the Training Centre in Oxford Street with his folder of newspaper clippings.

The following evening he procured the use of a photocopier and made duplicates of Jock's clippings, reports and photographs. He had to pay for the paper used.

On the Friday evening, as promised, he returned the folder to Jock Cameron before setting off north to his home and family. Cameron had thanked him and, holding up a finger told him, "I remember the name of one of the witnesses, Andrew. Laura Purdie's wee pal was called Alison, same name as my niece. I don't remember her surname but she stayed in Newton Mearns at the time and she was hoping to be a nurse when she left school, so she told me."

Fleming smiled to himself as he drove off. 'A fifteen year old girl called Alison from Newton Mearns in 1963 who had hopes of becoming a nurse. Aye, thanks a lot, Jock.'

SIX

Alison Swarbeck looked out at the falling snow and shivered. Her New York apartment was warm but the prospect of travelling in this kind of weather was worrying. So many things worried her now, life had made her that way. It seemed that she had always reached and grasped impulsively in her life and her impulses had seldom failed her. The omens had always been good, until now, the sun had always shone for her.

In September 1981, when Emma had turned five, Alison's parents had managed over for a whole month to visit Alison and see their granddaughter. They had looked so fit and well. Just three months ago she had spent ages on the telephone at Christmas talking to them both. Martin and Emma had spent time on the phone too.

Her older brother had called her yesterday to inform Alison that her mother was now in hospital following a heart attack at home. Her father was too distraught to call. She had called the hospital to enquire about her mother and Martin had spoken to the attending physician. They were hoping that Mrs Henderson would recover enough to permit surgery.

Alison had not seen her parents for two years although their health had seemed fine when she spoke to them on the phone. These circumstances served to emphasise just how remote they were. Tomorrow, if this snow would allow air travel, she hoped to see them again. Her friend from nursery care and Martin would manage to care for Emma. Her own hospital, her place of employment, were most understanding.

Andrew Fleming was back to his normal duties and had avoided any conversations with anyone on the subject of George Prentice's death. He knew that Campbell and MacKellar would have used his week's absence to bury the subject. He also knew that any further enquiry by himself would have to remain discreet as it would not be welcome. There would likely be anger and friction if he went near the Macraes. He went anyway.

On his way into the estate he saw a new car parked outside the estate house. It looked as if Gregor Mackay was at home so he stopped and went to the door. Gregor Mackay was amicable and explained his good spirits.

"My wife Laura is flying in tomorrow officer Fleming." he said with a broad smile. "She flew up from Florida to New York because there was some talk of a hurricane in Florida. Now that she has spent two days spending my money in New York she is finding it cold and now she is just coming home."

"That is good news." Fleming said. "I would like to meet this lady sometime."

Mackay's face turned serious.

"Not to talk about the painting, I hope."

"No, no." said Fleming, "your painting has always been a CID affair."

Mackay seemed relieved.

"Yes, I have told Sergeant Campbell that I do not want Laura to know about the painting. I am having it repaired."

"So I've heard." Fleming said. "No, that's none of my affair. I may have a question or two about the late Mr Fraser."

"What?" Mackay yelled, looking more serious now. "My wife was in Florida when that man met his death. In fact, I was with her. How can she possibly help with anything?"

"Because she wasn't always in Florida and he wasn't always dead." Fleming said firmly. He chose not to disclose the true identity of the dead man. It seemed from the lack of contradiction that Campbell had not told Mackay that his dead tenant had been one George Prentice.

"You have no need to interrogate my wife on that matter. What could you hope to achieve other than her distress? None of that is necessary, I forbid it." Mackay stormed.

Fleming looked squarely at Gregor Mackay.

"Interesting." he said evenly.

"What is interesting?" Mackay rasped in the same angry tone.

"Your attitude." Fleming said calmly. "None of your family even knew Arthur Fraser, right?"

"That's right. So we didn't concern ourselves with his living, so why should we concern ourselves with his dying? There is no need to be harassing our family over this matter." Mackay said in a quieter but more threatening voice.

"You are going to tell Mrs Mackay that the man died, right?" Fleming said.

"Of course." Mackay said stiffly.

"Good, Mr Mackay. I may still have to speak to her but I do not expect to be harassing her by doing so."

With that Fleming turned about and headed back to his car.

A couple of minutes later he drew in at the front of Macraes' cottage. Gordon Macrae opened the door and invited Fleming in to the lounge.

"You know that Gregor Mackay's home?" Fleming asked Gordon.

"Yes, I was down this morning." Gordon said with no suggestion of animosity. "His wife is supposed to be coming home tomorrow."

"What about your own wife, Mr Macrae? How is she?"

"Oh she takes to her bed in the afternoons, Constable Fleming. Her medication makes her tired."

"That's too bad." Fleming said sympathetically. "I don't suppose the business with the painting did anything to help."

"No, it didn't help her, as you say but anyway, it's back

now. He's getting it repaired apparently." Macrae said with his attractive lilt.

"Where did you grow up, Gordon?" Fleming asked with a smile.

"In Sutherland, on a croft." Gordon replied with evident pride.

"Not the sort of upbringing normally associated with the telling of lies." Fleming said, looking Gordon Macrae straight in the eye.

"No." Macrae replied in straight-faced agreement. "What are you getting at?"

"I am thinking that you would not willingly lie on your own account, Gordon, but even when you are trying to protect someone else, you find it hard to be convincing."

"What are you suggesting that I lied about?" Macrae asked, fidgeting a little.

"You never found that painting behind the Celtic cross, Gordon. There were acres of unbroken snow all around these crosses and no footprints, even after you claimed to have found the painting. That's the point, Gordon, you had possession of the painting. What you tried to explain away was how you came to have it."

Gordon Macrae dropped his head and stared at the carpet. There was a clicking sound as the door opened and the small figure of Elda Macrae in her dressing gown, entered the room.

"It's all right, Gordon. I'll tell the policeman the truth."

she said softly, her slipper clad feet shuffling to the armchair by the fire.

"It was all my doing, Constable. I accidentally damaged the painting when I was down there with Gordon. I realised how angry Mackay would be so I brought it straight up home to the cottage. Gordon didn't even know that I had done that. If Mackay found it damaged he would have blamed Gordon. He did that anyway."

"How did you come to damage it?" Fleming asked.

"I accidentally struck it with something that I had in my hand." she replied.

"The letter opener." Gordon Macrae interjected, making his wife turn angrily towards him. She chose not to say whatever she was thinking.

"Okay." said Fleming. "That's not actually my affair really but while we are in the mood to be telling the truth, Mrs Macrae, tell me about the man in the cottage over the back there."

The Macraes looked at each other as if wondering what to say or who should speak first. Elda Macrae turned to face Fleming.

"I never saw that man up close until the turn of the year just past. Gordon and I went round to visit him for the first time but he acted like he didn't want company so we just came away. I never went back and Gordon would never have gone back except he saw that there was no smoke from his chimney and that meant something was wrong. Well, we know now what was wrong."

"Did either of you recognise the man?" Fleming asked.

Again the Macraes looked at each other and again it was Elda who spoke.

"He was supposed to be Arthur Fraser and we've never known any Arthur Fraser, have we, Gordon?"

Gordon Macrae shook his head.

"Suppose for a moment that he wasn't called Arthur Fraser," Fleming said, "did you recognise him?" He was addressing Elda Macrae directly and he noticed how her fingers were locking and unlocking nervously on top of her knees.

"I didn't think he was Arthur Fraser." she replied. "I told Gordon how I felt after we had been round there. The guy acted creepy, as if he had something to hide."

"That's fair enough." Fleming said, opening his notebook. "I'll just make a wee note of your observations about Arthur Fraser, or whatever his name is. Now, Mrs Macrae, you are Elda Macrae but what was your maiden surname?"

He kept looking at his notebook and showed no reaction when she told him that her name had been 'Purdie' in a voice that reflected some tension. He ignored that and carried on to ask her age and repeated aloud what she was saying, as she recounted her suspicions of the man called Arthur Fraser.

As he returned his notebook to his pocket he asked, "Do either of you know Mrs Mackay and her daughter? They might well be home here tomorrow."

"Yes, we know them both quite well." Gordon Macrae replied honestly.

"Yes, they are both very nice." Elda Macrae agreed, losing any hint of her earlier tension.

"I am much obliged to both of you. It's been a pleasure meeting you." Fleming said with a smile. He had only just met Elda Purdie yet she was simply an older version of a 1963 newspaper photograph in his folder of copied documents at home. "Perhaps when you speak to Mrs Mackay you could mention that I would appreciate a word with her sometime."

Alison Swarbeck had not slept well but she was relieved to find that the snow had not continued overnight. There was a good chance her flight would go ahead as scheduled. To be on the safe side, she called the airline to have it confirmed before taking Emma to her friend Marion's apartment. Martin had left early for work that morning and hoped to collect Emma when he had finished. He had assured his wife that he and Marion would keep Emma safe while Alison was in Scotland.

Parting from Emma was difficult, especially so when she could not give the child any definite date for her return. That had been a problem with the flight booking too but the airline had given her a provisional return flight in two weeks' time and had promised to be as flexible as possible if her plans made this unsuitable.

She checked in at the airport and went for a coffee. It

was only ten o'clock in the morning but already she felt exhausted. She went to the washroom and threw some cold water over face in the hope of refreshing herself. It helped for the moment but as she walked around the shopping facilities she was still a little sore-headed and dazed.

Once aboard the aircraft she found herself in an aisle seat with two other women between herself and the window. The women spoke to each other in whispers and Alison could not hear what they were saying. It seemed to her tired mind that the whole plane was talking at once when all she wanted was peace and quiet. This flight held few positive emotions for her. When the plane lifted through the cloud and began to drift high above a floor of cotton wool, she was ready to sleep.

Alison awoke slowly and reluctantly. The women beside her had coffee cups, empty coffee cups, on the drop-down trays in front of them. A quick glance back along the aisle told Alison that the trolley had long gone. She closed her eyes again. She wasn't asleep and her ears were more acclimatised to the environment. The women beside her were talking about going home to their families. The woman next to her hadn't seen her husband and daughter since January apparently. Alison smiled to herself as she heard the accent and opened her eyes to look at the woman. "You're Scots, right?"

Fleming was in good humour as he returned with

Woman Police Constable Caroline Farmer and two men, brothers from Stirlingshire.

A newsagent's shop window had been broken during the night and a number of watches, lighters, pipes and wallets had been stolen from the display. In a hotel bar, some 50 yards away from the newsagent's, the manager of the hotel had been waiting patiently for four customers to finish their game of pool. The bar had closed but two of the men were regulars and he had no wish to offend them. The other two men were on holiday and staying at a guest house in the town. One of these men had a lapel badge with the name 'Ollie' on it. In due course all four had left the bar and the manager had been cleaning up when he heard the sound of breaking glass in the street outside.

Fleming had spoken to the local customers who confirmed that they had left the bar with the two men around three in the morning and the two brothers had gone off in the opposite direction. The locals were known to Fleming and he did not expect them to be the type to break windows. He had enquired in two neighbouring streets where practically every house was a guest house. In Sun Villa he and Constable Farmer had found the two brothers, still in bed. In plain sight in their room were the watches, lighters, pipes and wallets stolen from the newsagent's window. Hanging over the back of a chair was a jacket bearing a badge with the name 'Ollie' on it.

As they were placing the two brothers in custody at the

police office, Fleming explained to Douglas Campbell what had happened.

"It was all Caroline's work."

"Aye right." Campbell scoffed. "Oh by the way, Andy, some guy from Aberdeen phoned for you."

"Not Mackay?" Fleming asked.

"No, it wasn't Gregor Mackay. I left the name and phone number for you in the front office."

Fleming was surprised to see the name of John D. Turner again. This was the man who had bought the Mackays' former home in Aberdeen.

"Hello, Mr Turner, it's Andrew Fleming. What can I do for you?"

"I've been remembering what you said about anyone asking for Laura Turnbull or Laura Mackay. Well, there are still a few oilmen in the street here and I was speaking to one of them who stays a few doors away from me. He says that a couple of years back he had spoken to a strange looking guy with a suitcase. This fellow was looking for the Turnbulls and their daughter. My neighbour here knows George Turnbull and wondered if the guy might be a relative so he gave him the address for George Turnbull. He had told this guy that George's daughter had married and moved away. That seemed to come as a surprise to the man."

"That's good, Mr Turner, thank you. Do you have a name or a number for the man who was telling you this?"

"No. His name is Dave but I don't have his second name. I'll get it for you though."

"That would be a great help, thank you." Fleming said, trying not to sound disappointed.

"No problem, Officer Fleming. My brother was a cop in Austen."

The large group of senior gentlemen in overcoats formed a circle around the grave and the smaller group comprising immediate family. Detective Superintendent Johnston felt that he was attending more and more of these events every year. It had to be an age thing. The older one became the more people one knows and the more likely it is that you will know someone who dies. Today was just one more. He looked around the faces present and wondered who might be next. He reminded himself that something about today's burial was new to him. He had not been in Linn Cemetery before. He had been to the crematorium along the road but this cemetery burial was a first for him.

As the graveside service came to a close the group backed off towards the path and Johnston nodded to the two men he had brought with him. Like so many times before they had all known the deceased but had never met his family. While he walked at a reverend pace down the path James Johnston looked at the headstones he was passing. His attention was drawn to a small white headstone with black lettering. It was at odds with the other stones of granite or sandstone. The white marker was thinner and cheaper in appearance. It could well have been made from some sort of resin or crushed aggregate. Almost as an afterthought, Johnston looked at the name on the marker. It read, 'Laura Purdie, aged 15 years, daughter of Griselda Purdie, died 28th September 1963'.

James Johnston recalled recent conversations with Fleming and Cameron. This had to be the grave of the girl murdered by George Prentice.

There had never been a call from the individual mentioned by Margaret Rankine, a Mr Scott from the Probation Service. Fleming had been confident that Mrs Rankine would keep her promise to phone him. He called her, knowing that she had called and spoken to Douglas Campbell while Fleming had been in Glasgow. She knew by now that her brother had been identified as being the dead man at the cottage on Lauradale Estate.

"Mrs Rankine, have you ever spoken to that Probation Officer Scott that you told me about?"

"Well, I called to get him on that number that he gave me but all I got was Barlinnie Prison. They had no idea who Mr Scott was." she said sadly.

"Oh, I see." Fleming said slowly, not that he did see.

"Did your brother George ever write to you after you saw him at your house?" Fleming asked.

"No. He never wrote to me at any time." Mrs Rankine said positively.

"I only ask because it looks as if he considered doing so." Fleming explained. "He had begun a letter to you but had drawn a line through the few words he had written. I suspect that he wanted to explain matters to you but then decided that he couldn't write what he wanted to say. I saw it in his notepad."

"Really? You surprise me, Constable Fleming." Mrs Rankine said. "Can I see the letter?"

"When all the questions have been answered, Mrs Rankine, I will send it to you."

Fleming had no sooner put down the phone than Douglas Campbell came into the room, unusually closing the door behind him.

"It looks like your ideas about Prentice's death could be right, Andy. The blood test results have come back and the blood around the indent on the wall match Prentice's blood. The only blood injury he had was to the back of his head and that was the cause of death. Raymond Adam is livid apparently. I'm keeping out of the CID room in case the phone rings."

"I dare say." Fleming said without sympathy. "You won't escape him that easily, Dougie. He will be here pretty soon I imagine. You might be better to plan for that moment."

"I had stopped thinking about it, the death, I mean. I don't know where to start now."

"Have you still got the clothes from the cottage?" Fleming asked.

"Yes. I told his sister about them and invited her to pick them up but she hasn't been here yet."

"I never really looked at the suit in his wardrobe, Dougie, just through the pockets, but if Arthur Fraser went to the trouble of putting his initials on his suitcase maybe he did something of the kind with his suit."

"How could that help?" Campbell asked impatiently.

"Mrs Rankine can identify the suit and the suitcase as being in her brother's possession when he visited her but she has never met Arthur Fraser. To make the suppositions real we have to show that Prentice didn't just 'pick up' a suitcase somewhere that had once belonged to Arthur Fraser. That's what he told his sister. If he also has a suit that belonged to Arthur Fraser then he either killed or robbed Arthur Fraser to get it and it would be around the time of his death. Jack Kelly never saw any suitcase and if you were to ask, I just bet he never saw the suit."

"So who would want to kill Prentice?" Campbell asked with more impatience.

Fleming laughed. He knew that Campbell would dearly love for some informant to hand him the name of the culprit without his working to learn it for himself. He would love to save his own skin by having something to hand to DCI Adam when he arrived.

"Back to basics, I suppose, Dougie. Who would have motive and what motive? Revenge for Laura Purdie? Revenge for Arthur Fraser? Knowledge of the money in the suitcase?"

"I don't really see these as probable." Campbell said hopelessly.

"Yeah. Actually, I quite agree with you." Fleming said. "But someone had motive. That smack on the head was no accident. Someone hated the guy, either for a split second or for years."

"Right, I'll go and dig into that clothing." Campbell said as headed for the door. "I'd be better to be doing something when Adam arrives."

Fleming himself had no particular wish to be around when Raymond Adam arrived at the office. He set off on foot for the newsagent's shop where the window had been smashed. It would be repaired by now and he needed to know the cost of that repair. He also wanted to know some other things.

As he reached the top of the High Street he was stopped by a well-dressed woman in her forties.

"I think you may be Constable Fleming." she said with a look of expectation in her eyes.

"Yes, I am. How can I help you?" Fleming replied, aware that he had never seen the woman in his life before.

"Elda Macrae has described you to me." the woman explained. "She has told me that you want to speak to me. I am Laura Mackay."

"Oh, I see. Well, in that case I do want to speak to you. You have been told about the death of the man in the cottage? The man you knew as Arthur Fraser?"

Laura Mackay nodded.

"My husband and Elda have both told me. Gregor doesn't want me to be talking to the police about it, I don't know why. He gets so angry." she said as if her husband's anger was something she had become used to. "What could I tell you about the dead man? I didn't speak to him or even get close to him in all the time he was at Lauradale."

Fleming noticed how Mrs Mackay had not responded to his suggestion that the 'dead man' was only known as Arthur Fraser.

"Would the same be true for your daughter, Lorna?" Fleming asked.

"As far as I know," Mrs Mackay said pointedly. "She wouldn't go near him, I'm sure."

"Have you discussed the man with Elda Macrae?"

For the first time, Laura Macrae looked down before answering.

"We have spoken about how spooky the man was. Elda was sure the man was hiding some secret. I suppose she had a point. He did act a bit weird."

"All right, Mrs Mackay, thank you for introducing yourself to me. I know that your husband wouldn't want me coming to your house to speak to you but it may be helpful to have your cooperation if further questions arise. He may well receive another visit from the CID. They are looking seriously at this death now."

Mrs Mackay looked troubled by this information.

"Would there be any way that I could contact you privately Constable Fleming? If Gregor should go to Aberdeen …"

Fleming smiled and reached into his pocket for a small

notepad. He wrote down a number on the top sheet and tore it off to give to Mrs Mackay.

"My home number. If there is no reply, you can leave a message."

Fleming was glad to get finished and go home to Mary and the children. The atmosphere in the office had certainly deteriorated after Raymond Adam had arrived. MacKellar and Adam had never been branches of the same tree. They could easily disagree on matters far less substantial than a disregarded murder. There was a great deal of shouting behind closed doors. Campbell had been told to spend his evening on duty, catching up on lost time, briefing Adam on every known item of the enquiry into the death of George Prentice.

Adam had told MacKellar that he had seen immediately from the subsequent report submitted by Fleming that 'the man had the good sense to be taking no responsibility for their neglect'.

Tomorrow Raymond Adam and Douglas Campbell would go to Lauradale and 'do what the CID should have been doing in the first place'.

Andrew Fleming waited until the children were in bed before taking out the folder of press cuttings, copied from those of Jock Cameron. He poured himself a glass of malt and dry ginger and settled down to scour the papers in search of anything he might have missed in relation to the trial of George Prentice.

He had been over these before at Oxford Street Training Centre and at home, but now he felt closer to the original case and those involved.

There, at the start of the trial was Elda Purdie who had last seen her daughter Laura as the girl had left to attend the fairground. She had described to the court what her daughter had been wearing at that time. According to her testimony she had next seen her daughter at the mortuary where she had identified the girl prior to post-mortem.

The dead girl's friend had testified that she had met Laura at the fairground and had spent time with her before she and Laura had become separated. It appeared that Laura had left the fairground without telling her friend, Alison Henderson, that she was leaving. The fifteen years old witness had not seen Laura Purdie again but could describe her clothing that day. She had told the court that Laura was in possession of money and cigarettes.

Fleming marked this part of the report with a large 'X'. He realised that Alison Henderson was the young girl referred to by Jock Cameron as 'Alison from Newton Mearns who wanted to be a nurse'. He noticed too that no defence pressure had been put on either of these first two witnesses.

More pressure had been applied to the witnesses employed at the fairground. The man who ran the 'Waltzer' and had watched the couple from his central 'office' on the ride was 60 years of age at the time. The 'office' was an enclosed hub fitted with a small glass window. Beneath the glass was a gap where other workers returned the takings for him to tote up and provide change when needed. The 'office' and the surrounding boardwalk remained still while the undulating surface of the ride was in motion. The boss man had nothing to do while the ride was in motion except look out at those on the boardwalk and ensure that the music kept playing.

It would be natural, the prosecution had argued, for the witness to pay attention to a pretty teenage girl dressed in the manner described by the earlier witnesses. With nothing better to do, the witness from the 'Waltzer' had watched the girl take two cigarettes from a twenty packet and give one to a young man next to her, a man who looked to be eight to ten years older, he had thought. The girl had then lit both cigarettes with a lighter that the man had taken from her 'as if it belonged to him.'

The witness described this lighter as being the same type that he owned himself. He had produced his own lighter and agreed that it matched the cigarette lighter in evidence, the difference in the court exhibited lighter being the brass case and the letters GP engraved on the top.

The young girl had snatched the lighter back from him in what the witness described as a bit of a 'carry-on' between them.

Asked in court if he could identify the young man he had seen with the girl, he identified the accused, George Prentice. When the girl had been reported as missing and her photograph had appeared in the newspapers he had recognised her. He confirmed that he was certain it was the girl he had seen with the accused and had reported as much to the police.

The defence counsel had questioned everything the witness had said. The man wore thick glasses and his eyesight was questioned as to how he could see and be certain of what he had seen, when he wore such thick glasses. His reply was simply that he had been wearing them at the time.

The next witness, a sixteen year old youth called Thomson, had not seen the girl at any time but had seen a man, aged in his twenties, staggering from the woods about a mile from the fairground. The man had looked out of breath from running and he was muttering to himself. Thomson could not hear what he was saying. When asked what happened next the boy reported a loud scream from deep in the woods and he had run away. The young man identified the accused George Prentice as the man who had emerged from the wood. Despite rigorous cross-examination the young Thomson had held firm to his evidence.

Fleming reflected on the evidence given by the boy Thomson. Jock Cameron had not placed much weight on the fact that Prentice was already out of the woods when a scream was heard. Fleming did not readily accept that someone sufficiently affected by finding the body as to scream at the top of their voice would then turn tail and refrain from telling someone about their discovery. Another big cross was inserted at this part of the report.

The witnesses Thomson and Henderson were relatively young when this event happened twenty-one years before. Could they be traceable?

The woman at the candy floss stand had been the last to see the accused and Laura Purdie as they stopped at her stand for the man to buy a candy floss for the girl. They had then left the fairground together and walked in the general direction of the wood, 'but not necessarily going there'. According to the witness, the girl was under no coercion to accompany the man, the man she identified as being George Prentice, the man in the dock.

The body had been found a week later, face down in brown leaves behind a large tree. Laura Purdie was still clothed as described by her mother and her friend but was not wearing either tights or knickers. These items had not been found. The girl's shoes had been nearby and the lighter, the one produced in court, was several feet from her. Her jacket pockets had contained no money or cigarettes despite the evidence of witnesses that she had those things in her possession.

The medical examiner had described how death had been caused by manual strangulation from the front, using both hands. The body bore heavy bruising to the front lower chest and abdomen and there was evidence of rape in the form of bruising to her inner thighs. She had not been virgo intacta prior to the assault but the police surgeon had been satisfied that sexual intercourse had been forcefully carried out by the assailant.

Fleming wondered at the fact that Laura had been found face-down when all the attack, including the rape, had been face-on, according to the medical evidence. Jock had told him of the fingernail impressions yet there was no mention of these in the reported press coverage of the trial. There was no report of defence injuries or any evidence of the girl resisting at all.

Reading the various reports of the closing arguments, Fleming considered that the defence had not capitalised on the lack of convincing evidence of the actual crimes libelled. They had not rebuffed the prosecution assumption that whoever raped the girl had also murdered her.

For whatever reason, this assumption had been left to be taken as read. The defence had helped to consolidate this assumption by raising the concession of sorts, by the medical examiner, that strangulation could well have been part of the assailant's controlling measures over the girl. His evidence therefore was binding the crimes together as simultaneous and the defence had not tried to shake them apart. They had rather meekly accepted prosecution assumptions and their own client was telling them nothing to guide them out of it.

"Not necessarily simultaneous." Fleming thought as he closed the folder. He thought briefly about Prentice and his lack of cooperation in the rape and murder investigation and how that must have given his defence a poor hand to play. Prentice had not knowingly discussed his situation with anyone and now the man was dead. His silence had cost him an eighteen year sentence. Why would he stay silent when accused of the rape and murder of a fifteen year old girl?

SEVEN

The next day was spent quietly at work. Fleming wrote up reports and statements at the office while Detective Chief Inspector Adam and Detective Sergeant Campbell pursued enquiries at Lauradale with the Macraes and the Mackays.

The telephone rang beside him and he lifted it to hear the voice of his old friend James Johnston.

"J.J., how are you?"

"I'm fine thanks, Andy. I'm just calling to let you know a couple of things about the Prentice case." Johnston began. "Quite by accident, I discovered the grave of Laura Purdie in the Linn Cemetery. The headstone is some cheap affair but it describes the dead girl as being the 'daughter of Griselda Purdie'.

Johnston paused to allow this to be absorbed by Fleming.

"Last night I read over the coverage of the trial, Jim. Nowhere does it mention the girl's mother as Griselda Purdie, only as Elda Purdie. Makes me wonder about that lighter?" Fleming responded.

"I asked Jock Cameron if he had known that the

woman's proper name was Griselda. He says she never told him that and everybody he spoke to referred to her as Elda, so that was what she was reported under."

"Well, he's right about that." Fleming said. "Even her husband refers to her as Elda. What was the other thing you were going to tell me, Jim?"

I was talking to an old snitch the other day, Andy. I just met the guy in the street and I asked him if he had known George Prentice from his days inside. He remembered him as the guy who killed the young lassie and asked what I wanted to know. I told him that Prentice was dead and he laughed. I asked him what was funny about that and he told me that Prentice should have died seven years ago when Sonny Thomson stabbed him in prison."

"Who is 'Sonny' Thomson?" Fleming asked.

"You read about the trial, remember the young boy who had seen George Prentice staggering out of the woods? That was Sonny Thomson." the Detective Superintendent said with satisfaction.

"Why would he stab Prentice?" Fleming asked.

"He was just a fifteen year old boy when he saw Prentice running out the woods. His story was that he heard a scream and ran away. In 1968 the same wee boy was twenty and in prison for serious assault as a gang member. According to the snitch Thomson did it for macho reasons, you know, 'I'm the big man now. I did nothing but run away then but I'm doing my bit now', sort of thing. Prentice almost died apparently and Thomson wasn't even suspected. We can't question him about it now though. He died in a motor bike accident last year."

Fleming thanked his old friend and explained how Raymond Adam was now leading Campbell by the nose through the murder enquiry.

"I don't suppose Raymond is making many friends." Johnston remarked.

"No." Fleming agreed. "MacKellar is upstairs right now sticking pins in a Ray Adam doll.

What J.J. had told him made Fleming think about the Prentice murder case again and it was pointless trying to concentrate on his report writing. He put the paperwork aside and headed out to the newsagent's shop where he and Caroline had recently cleared up the theft from the window. He asked the newsagent if he happened to have any of the old style petrol lighters. The newsagent reached beneath the counter and produced a chromed version.

"Like this."

"Yes, like that but in brass if you have one." Fleming asked. After some searching the newsagent found a brass lighter. With the look of a man who had just dropped his dentures down the toilet, Fleming paid for the lighter.

"They are all collector's items now." the newsagent explained.

Fleming took the lighter down the street to the cobbler's shop where he asked 'old George' to engrave the initials, 'GP', on the lid of the lighter. 'Old George' was not so very old but he had named his son George so had suffered the indignity of being 'old George' ever since.

"Well, there was a lady with a motive." Raymond Adam remarked as he and Campbell drove away from the Macrae home. They had elicited from Elda Macrae that she was the mother of Laura Purdie, the child victim, whose murder had put Prentice in prison to spend eighteen years behind bars.

"She's the only one we know about." Campbell replied. "But is she capable? Would her husband have been prepared to do that for her?"

"I honestly don't see either of them as strong candidates, Douglas. If anything, that couple want to put the past behind them. At their age, I can understand that better."

"The Mackays seem even less likely to have been involved." Campbell said with some relish. Perhaps now, Adam was beginning to see the sense of not pursuing the murder too intently.

"Yes, but that business with the painting is strange. Gregor Mackay strikes me as a covetous, possessive individual, yet he wants to draw a veil over the theft of his valuable painting to protect his wife from police enquiry. Why would his wife be distressed when she is not a suspect? What is his concern? On the death of George Prentice, he simply claims not to have known the man as anyone but some Arthur Fraser from Glasgow and to quote him, he was 'a million miles away at the time'."

"That's right. We already knew that and Mrs Mackay has only just come home to learn of the man's death. She seemed to be genuinely upset by it though." Campbell remarked.

"The daughter Lorna has been at university in Aberdeen and has never seen the man they knew as Arthur Fraser. So Mackay says. He seemed keen to keep his daughter out of it." Adam remembered.

"Do you think we need to see her?" Campbell asked as if he agreed with Mackay.

"She probably does have an alibi, but we need to be sure that she has, Douglas. The CID in Aberdeen can check it out for us."

Campbell smiled and nodded.

Almost a week went by with Raymond Adam still around each day. Fleming had chosen to stay out of his way and he was not consulted at any point. Nevertheless, before he left Corran Bay, Raymond Adam came to say 'Goodbye' to Fleming.

"I am not a great deal wiser on this murder." Adam told Fleming. "But I am just as sure as I ever was that your opinion on this death is the right one. Too much time was wasted at the start trying to give me all that evasive crap. What I cannot put in one personality however, is the motive, physical capability and opportunity. I am going to have to leave this one for the time being. There is too much going on down on my own patch."

"So what is happening with the George Prentice death?" Fleming asked. "It is still a murder enquiry?"

"Yes, of course. I agree with Mr MacKellar that nobody wants an unsolved murder case on their books but we can't dispose of it just by calling it something else."

He had said this with a twisted smile on his face. He enjoyed disagreeing with MacKellar.

"If you hear of anything useful, Andrew, I will happy to hear from you."

When he arrived home that evening Mary had a message for him.

"A lady called Laura Mackay phoned for you, Andrew. She said it would be in order for you to call on her at home tomorrow afternoon. I hope this is not some kind of affair, you have started." she said with a smile.

"No dear, she is just telling me that her husband will not be at home to object."

Mary turned sharply.

"So, it is an affair?"

"No, don't be silly. She is a witness who wants to avoid her husband hearing what she has to say. That is what she meant."

"She doesn't know that tomorrow is your day off, then?" Mary said a little sarcastically.

"She would have no way of knowing that unless you told her."

"It wouldn't make a difference anyway, would it? You would still go." Mary said from experience.

"In some ways it might be better that I am off." Fleming said earnestly. "Don't suppose you want to come with me?"

"Now who's being silly?"

The following afternoon Fleming headed for Lauradale dressed in sports jacket and flannels. This allowed him an inside pocket to carry his notebook. In another pocket he had a small camera.

Laura Mackay greeted him with a smile.

"Come in, Constable Fleming. I assume you are not on duty today?"

"No, but today is suitable, is it not?"

"Gregor has gone back to Aberdeen. He is blazing mad at having to be around for these men from the CID. According to him he has lost so much working time but I doubt that he would have stayed here if it was more important for him to be elsewhere."

"It would not be pleasant for anyone, I suppose, but Gregor would have little to say in response to their questions." Fleming suggested.

"Oh he had nothing to offer. 'I wasn't there. End of story' was about all he said. He wouldn't have been here certainly."

"What did the CID have to say about the dead man's identity?" Fleming asked.

"Well, that is all out in the open now, Mister Fleming. No more Arthur Fraser, it was George Prentice."

"Has that affected anyone?" Fleming asked seriously.

"I suppose it has. Elda is terribly upset by it. You know of course that George was convicted of her daughter's death?"

"He was convicted of her daughter's rape and murder back in 1964." Fleming said, fairly certain that Adam would have disclosed as much.

"Yes, he was but Elda actually saw very little of him back then. She had her suspicions about the man in the cottage being someone other than who he was claiming to be. I don't know if it was a Glasgow streetwise thing or just woman's intuition, but she knew him from somewhere. She admitted to me that she had tried to break into Gregor's filing cabinet to find out who he might be. That's when she tore my painting." she said with a laugh that suggested that Laura cared little about the damage. "Gregor tells me that it is away to be cleaned. I am sure he means well."

"How long have you known this? Did you tell the CID?" Fleming asked, smiling at his host's humour.

"No, I didn't tell them." she said as if excusing herself. "I only found out this morning when I took Elda to the doctor."

"She is that bad?" Fleming asked with concern.

"I don't know that. She had an appointment."

"Is Gordon unwell?"

"No, but he isn't there, that's why I was the one taking Elda to the surgery. Gregor has gone to some solicitors in Inverness about forthcoming legislation on crofting rights. That is what bothers me." Laura Mackay said with some concern.

"Why would that bother you, Mrs Mackay?"

"Because it looks as if Elda made her appointment after knowing that Gordon would be away. That would not normally be the case or even necessary, if you see what I mean. She knew he was going to Inverness and asked me if I could possibly take her."

"I see." said Fleming.

Laura Mackay moved to sit on the settee beside Fleming and spoke quietly of how Elda Macrae had confided in her since coming to Lauradale. Elda had told Laura of the younger days when life had been rough for Elda. Her drinking habit had developed before she had given birth to her daughter. There had been no father for the child and her own parents were in no position to help even if they had been so inclined.

"Did she tell you then just who she really was?" Fleming asked.

"Not as regards the murder of her daughter. She had not told Gordon about her having a daughter so it was a fragile subject and one to be avoided. I was never told until this morning that Elda's daughter had been murdered and of course it was George who had done it. The CID knew obviously and I think Elda realised that it might be a good time to clear the air. It wasn't to be a secret anymore. She had never told Gordon, about the murder, I mean. In all these years of marriage she had never told Gordon. Despite that he knew the truth about the girl's death. Apparently he had figured it out for himself and chose not to raise it. She told me that this morning too."

"So now you know all about Elda Purdie. Does she know all about you?" Fleming asked, aware of the gamble he was taking.

"What do you mean?" Laura Mackay asked with her first serious expression of the afternoon.

Fleming reached into his inside pocket and took out his notebook. From the notebook he removed the five by three photograph of a young girl, the photograph that had been in Prentice's bedside frame. He handed it to her.

"Twice in the last half hour you have referred to George Prentice as 'George'. You are the first person I have heard doing that." Fleming said.

Laura Mackay's eyes opened wide and her jaw dropped as she brought her hands up to her cheeks and asked, "Where on earth did you get that?"

"It was the only photograph he owned." Fleming said poignantly. He saw Laura's eyes begin to moisten.

"All these years," she whispered. "The Locarno Ballroom. How did you know Mister Fleming?"

"I can still see a likeness but the real reason lies in what makes sense, Mrs Mackay. There is coincidence in you and Elda having a Glasgow background but when George

147

Prentice joins you here and is prepared to live in that cold, damp cottage, that cannot be mere coincidence. He did not come here to live the existence he has been living unless he had strong reasons for doing so. He is just not the type to be here without a motive. You were the motive. Did you know it was him?"

Laura Mackay was crying now.

"He has been here since 1982 and I hardly saw him. He just stayed hidden but in the summer he became bolder and would move closer. I saw him at a distance. He reminded me a bit of George but I never seriously thought it could be him after all these years. I suppose I didn't really know until the CID confirmed it the other day."

"Had you mentioned your suspicions to anyone?"

"To Gregor? Oh Lord no, he would have gone ballistic."

"To anyone?" Fleming reminded her of the question asked.

"Well, I did actually. We were in Florida at Christmas and, as you might expect, I was on the phone to mum and dad in Aberdeen. I told my father about the creepy guy who was staying on the estate and of how he reminded me of George Prentice."

"Your dad knows George Prentice?" Fleming interrupted.

"Yes. He knows of him from years ago in Glasgow." Laura Mackay answered cautiously. Her caution was not lost on Fleming.

"What was your dad's response?"

"He was angry but he doesn't rage like Gregor. He said there was chance it could be George, right enough. I've no idea what he meant by that but he made me swear not to tell mum. He would sort things out somehow."

"Do you think he has?" Fleming prompted.

"Goodness no, mister Fleming, my father is not fit to come down here in winter, let alone attack someone half his age when he arrives. No, no, right sentiment but the wrong man, I'm afraid."

"Would Gordon Macrae have known who that guy really was?" Fleming wondered aloud.

"I doubt it. It would be against everything that Gordon stands for to be doing such a thing. He would still be blushing with guilt to this day, he's that honest." Again Laura sounded confident in her defence.

"When did your daughter go back to university?" Fleming asked without menace.

"About the seventh of January. Why do you ask?"

"Is she not about due a break?" Fleming said in the manner of one who had no way of knowing when the universities broke up.

"The mid-term, yes. She could be down this weekend, in fact. You don't suspect Lorna, do you? She had an exam the day George Prentice is supposed to have died."

"I did not suspect Lorna, exam or no exam." Fleming said with a smile. "And you were still in Florida, weren't you?"

"Damn right I was." she replied with confidence.

"I don't suppose you know any nurses called Alison, do you?" Fleming asked with no expectations of a positive response.

"As a matter of fact, I recently met one. She works in New York."

"That isn't her then," Fleming said, throwing his hands up in mock disappointment. "The one I want to find is from Newton Mearns."

"You are joking." she said, losing her own smile. "The one I met was sitting beside me on the plane from New York. She is a nurse called Alison and she was going home to Newton Mearns because her mother is ill in the Victoria Infirmary." Laura Mackay told him

"What sort of age is this Alison?" Fleming asked.

"Late thirties, forty, maybe."

"Did she tell you her surname by any chance?"

"Yes she did but she is married and I don't remember the name now. Her mother's name is Henderson, so she told me, if that helps." Laura suggested.

"I think you may just have delivered the biggest coincidence of them all." Fleming said, shaking his head in disbelief.

"Will Gregor be home this weekend?" he asked as he rose to make his departure.

"You want to speak to Lorna, don't you?"

Fleming sighed.

"Are there subjects I should avoid? Does she know?"

"She knows that Gregor is not her biological father if that is what you are getting at, Mister Fleming. She just doesn't know who her real father was." Laura Mackay said in serious tones.

"Nothing to be gained by raising that, but I would ask her, as I have done with everyone, how well she may have known the man in the cottage. I can learn what I want to know without telling Lorna things she doesn't need to know, Mrs Mackay."

"I will ring you if this weekend looks suitable, Mr Fleming. At the moment I do not know who to expect."

When Fleming arrived home he was treated to more sarcasm from Mary who wanted to know how his 'date' had gone.

"Actually, it went better than I expected." Fleming told her. "Do you fancy a trip to Glasgow tomorrow?"

"If I did it would be to a shop," she replied. "I can't imagine you being game for that."

"I'll put up with it if you allow me to visit the Victoria Infirmary." Fleming said seriously.

"I'm needing to get something to wear at my brother's wedding." she said warily.

Fleming groaned.

"I'll drop you off and pick you up after my hospital visit."

Gordon Macrae had listened patiently to the solicitor

and after an hour was not much better informed than he had been by the magazine article that had prompted his appointment. The article promised more than the solicitor was suggesting was currently possible. The outlook for crofters like himself, was still 'fluid' but progressive. There was judicial interest in securing rights for crofting communities and in modernising their rights according to varying criteria. How this might affect Gordon personally could not yet be assessed. He had brought such papers as he had retained from the croft and had lodged them with the solicitor. He left the solicitor's office with an assurance that his interests would be pursued as the proposals became law.

Patience had always been a dominant virtue for Gordon and he held no great hopes of wealth. His name was on some list or other and his forebears had worked hard for his right to put it there. They deserved to be acknowledged in the same way as the others.

Now he would make his way home to Elda. She had been badly affected by the visit of the CID boss and the whole business of her daughter's death being raised again. His wife had not realised that the Arthur Fraser character had actually been George Prentice, the man accused and convicted of her daughter's death. Elda was not as strong as she had once been and Gordon hoped that she had not resorted to the bottle the minute his back was turned.

His concerns were unfounded. Elda Macrae was indeed shaken by the events of recent days, including this day, but she had not even considered alcohol. When she heard Gordon's car drawing up outside she hurriedly placed the white appointment card into her handbag and went out to meet her husband.

Fleming went to the Victoria Infirmary and enquired as to the whereabouts of Mrs Henderson from Newton Mearns. He was told the ward to go to and given directions. He was also given instructions to speak to the Ward Sister before going into the ward.

Having found the ward and the Ward Sister, busy in her office, Fleming asked her if Mrs Henderson was still on the ward.

"Are you family?" the Sister asked, looking quite stern.

"No. I am not family and it is not actually the patient I want to speak to. I need to speak to her daughter Alison on an important matter."

"Oh really," the Sister said without losing any of her serious demeanour. "Alison is already speaking to her mother on a serious matter. Mrs Henderson is being moved shortly to the Royal Infirmary for surgery. Alison and her father are speaking to her at the moment."

"Of course." Fleming said submissively. "How long might it be before her mum leaves here?"

"In the next half hour, I expect. What is your business with her daughter?"

"I am a police officer, Sister, my name is Andrew Fleming. I have a few questions to ask Alison Henderson but I will first have to make sure that she is the same Alison Henderson who gave evidence to the High Court in 1964. She was fifteen then and had hopes of becoming a nurse."

The Sister considered this and smiled.

"If you take a seat in the waiting room opposite, I will ask her if she wants to speak with you. I'll explain which Alison Henderson you are looking for."

Fleming sat in the small room where the silence was broken only by the ticking of a clock. He pictured his wife Mary trying on different brightly coloured outfits for her brother's wedding, totally oblivious of any clock on the wall. Ten minutes later the door was pushed open and an attractive woman in her late thirties, entered the room.

"Mr Fleming? I am Alison Swarbeck. I used to be Alison Henderson." She extended her hand.

"How do you do, Mrs Swarbeck?" Fleming said, shaking her hand gently. "I can only apologise for this terrible intrusion. I had only a few clues as to where I might find you. How is your mum? I hear she is going to the Royal?"

"Yes, she is stronger than she was a week ago but they want to carry out a cardiac procedure to improve matters for the longer term. Exactly what is to be done is a matter for the surgeons at the Royal Infirmary to decide."

"Well the Royal is the right place for that, I believe. Now Alison, can I first check that you are the Alison Henderson who gave evidence in the trial of George Prentice at Glasgow High Court in 1964?"

Alison looked suddenly sad.

"My friend, Laura, my best friend was raped and murdered. That was a nightmare." she said slowly and painfully.

Fleming was relieved to have found the right Alison.

"How well do you remember that day, the last day you saw Laura Purdie?" Fleming asked.

Alison came out of her memory lock to ask, "You are a policeman, right, not a reporter?"

Fleming smiled and brought his warrant card from his inside pocket along with his notebook. He showed the card to Alison.

"You were spoken to back then by a detective called Jock Cameron. You told him you wanted to be a nurse someday. Am I right?"

"Yes. I am a nurse now, in New York." she said with pride.

"So I am told but I knew nothing else about you except that you were from Newton Mearns and your mum was in the Victoria Infirmary." Fleming explained. "Now the case against George Prentice – you never knew him did you?"

"No. I never saw him at all before the trial." Alison answered frankly enough.

"And the witness Thomson, a boy your own age, did you know him?"

"No. I never even saw him at the trial but he was mentioned in the newspaper I remember the name."

"Now Alison, you do remember meeting Laura. How was she dressed?"

Alison developed her memory stare again.

"She had on her denim jacket and a white polo neck sweater. She was wearing a shiny black, pretend leather miniskirt, tights and black shoes. She was made up too, lipstick, rouge, hair lacquer, 'the works'," Alison smiled at the memory.

"Would her mother be happy to let her go out like that?" Fleming asked with a smile.

"She was raging." Alison said with a smile that quickly faded. She had said it before realising what she had said.

"How do you know that?" Fleming asked, having noticed Alison's change of expression.

Alison looked down at the floor and continued to look down as she spoke in shameful voice.

"Laura's mother told the court that she had last seen her daughter as she left to go to the fairground. Laura told me that her mother was lying on the couch asleep when she left. She stole money, cigarettes and a lighter from her mother while Mrs Purdie was sleeping off her drink. She showed me these things."

"So the cigarettes, the money and the lighter all belonged to her mother. Maybe the make-up too? Did the lighter have initials on it, Alison?"

Alison raised her head again.

"Yes. It had initials on it."

"What brand were the cigarettes?"

"Embassy tipped, I think."

"And the money? How much?"

"A pound note, a ten shilling note and some change. Old money, like."

"You never told the court about that did you, Alison, why?"

"I was afraid. My mother had told me not to be a chatterbox in court. I was just to answer what I was asked and I wasn't actually asked about the lighter having initials. Nobody had ever mentioned the lighter."

Fleming nodded. He could assume that 'nobody' included Jock Cameron.

"So, Laura left the house with her mother flaked out on the couch?"

"That's what she told me." Alison agreed.

"So, how did you know that her mum was raging, as you put it? You saw her, didn't you?"

Alison looked down at the floor again.

"I know that you never told the court Alison. You have explained why. If you were never asked then you were not obliged to say. That is not your fault, your mum was right about that, but I am asking you now. I don't know if it will change anything but the truth is always best. Tell me about Mrs Purdie's rage please."

Alison lifted her head. There were tears in her eyes now.

"She came to the fair. I thought she was still drunk and obviously very angry. She shouted and swore at me but it had all to do with Laura. 'That little bitch stole from me, her own mother' and 'wait 'til I get a hold of that girl. I'll teach her to steal from her mother' and so on. I told her that Laura wasn't there anymore and she stormed off but I never saw where she went." Alison wiped her eyes.

"Had you met Mrs Purdie before?" Fleming asked.

"Yes, quite a few times but never for very long. Just when I went to her house to get Laura or when she came to my house to collect her.

"Did she come to your house the next day, like you told the court?" Fleming asked.

"Yes. She did. She was sober then." Alison remembered.

"Was she anxious or still annoyed?" Fleming asked.

"She spoke more to my mum actually, but I thought she sounded worried. Of course my mum was worried too. I got the life questioned out of me as to where Laura might have gone but I had really had no idea. I never told my mum about Mrs Purdie being drunk the day before or about Laura stealing her things."

"Did Mrs Purdie have long fingernails in these days, Alison, or do you not remember?"

"Yes, I remember." Alison said with a smile. "She had long nails alright and they were usually painted in some hideous colour."

Fleming had just entered contact numbers and addresses for Alison into his notebook when the door was pushed open by an elderly gentleman in a suit.

"That's your mum ready to go the Royal now Alison. Maybe you want to say 'Goodbye' until this evening."

"Of course, Dad."

Fleming smiled at the older man before telling Alison, "Thank you very much, Alison. I am sorry to have met you under these circumstances but I wish your mum all the best at the Royal."

"That's kind, Mr Fleming. How did you know about me?"

"From your friend, Laura. Your recent friend, Laura, who sat beside you on the plane from New York." Fleming said with a smile

"Really? That's amazing. She was such a nice lady. She hadn't seen her husband and daughter since the start of the year."

"Is that so?"

Fleming set off for work the next day having heard the description of the wedding outfit, having seen it modelled by Mary, having heard of every other outfit that 'might have done' and those that 'just wouldn't do'. It was raining and he was backshift but he was still glad to be going to work.

There was a note waiting for him to call a Dave Burnett at a certain number. So he did.

"Mr Burnett? Andrew Fleming. How can I help you?"

"Hello Constable Fleming. I think you were speaking to Texas John Turner at No. 34 and he asked me about strangers asking for Laura Turnbull."

"Right, Mr Burnett, so you are the Dave that he mentioned."

"Yes, that's correct."

"So, I was enquiring with John about anyone who might have been asking for an address for Laura Turnbull."

"Well, a couple of years ago now, there was a guy in the street who asked me which house was the Mackays'. He was quite rough and he was carrying a suitcase. He did seem to know Laura because he could tell me that she had moved from Glasgow to Aberdeen in 1962. He already knew that her parents lived in Brent Avenue but he would prefer not to speak to them. I told him that Laura and her husband and daughter had moved to some place on the west coast. He asked me if anyone else had been asking about Laura recently. I told him that I had heard of someone but I never saw the man."

"Do you still have George Turnbull's address and telephone number?" Fleming asked.

"I do indeed. It's 22 Brent Avenue and the phone number ..." he was obviously looking up the number as he spoke and eventually found it.

"Was there anything else this man said to you, Mr Burnett?"

"He asked me how long Laura had been married and he wanted to know her daughter's name. I'm not absolutely certain that that was his question but he did ask me something about the daughter."

"You have been very helpful, Mr Burnett. Thank you."

160

"There was that Probation Officer guy." Burnett began afresh. "He was interested in where Laura Mackay had gone too. I told him about the rough man with the suitcase and he said he was trying to trace that man. 'Had this untidy man given me his name?' he asked. Well he hadn't so that was that."

"Did the Probation Officer give you his name?" Fleming asked.

"Somebody Scott, I think. He showed me a card."

"I am most grateful to you and Mr Turner. If that question about the daughter occurs to you, perhaps you could let me know what it was. Thanks again for your help."

It seemed that the mysterious Mr Scott had progressed from speaking to Mrs Rankine in Falkirk up to learning about the Mackays from Mr Burnett in Aberdeen.

The weather was beginning to improve and Fleming walked up the High Street to the newsagent's shop.

"You are becoming a regular." the newsagent joked.

"How much are twenty Embassy tipped?" Fleming asked, reaching reluctantly into his pocket.

"You've bought a lighter and now cigarettes, but you don't even smoke." the newsagent joked again. "Why?"

"I simply have too much money." Fleming said sarcastically.

As he walked back down the street he saw Mrs Mackay about to enter a coffee shop of good repute with other women of a similar age. Fleming could see how this might be a regular rendezvous.

When she saw him, Laura Mackay stopped and raised a forefinger in acknowledgement.

"Saturday morning, Mr Fleming, would that be okay?"

"Yes, thank you. About ten?"

"Whenever." she replied.

Fleming was happy to keep his enquiries 'out of hours' and Saturday morning would allow him to excuse himself from shopping.

When he returned to the office he found Darren Black on duty and took the opportunity of speaking to him alone. From Darren he hoped to learn what progress DCI Adam and DS Campbell were making in the George Prentice murder enquiry.

"I have kept myself out of it to be honest, Andy, but Dougie seemed to be gloating over Raymond Adam's failure to shed light on who might have killed Prentice. I heard Dougie telling MacKellar that Gregor Mackay had a lot to say about the death of someone he claimed not to have known. Mackay had told Campbell and Adam that he had only ever spoken to Prentice, or 'Fraser' as he calls him, when the man wanted to install his own central heating. Yet he was able to complain that the man had been spying on his wife and daughter through binoculars. His wife had apparently told her own father about this too."

"How would he know that?" Fleming asked sharply.

"I don't know. Maybe she told her husband or maybe he was there when she called her father." Black suggested.

"According to Mrs Mackay she was purposefully avoiding a situation where her husband could overhear her conversation with her father about Prentice. She feared the reaction she could expect." Fleming said confidently. He chose not to suggest that Darren had given him food for thought. Perhaps Gregor Mackay had been present when Laura had spoken to her father about Prentice, but present at the other end of the line. Alison Henderson seemed to think that, contrary to common belief, Gregor Mackay had not been seen by Laura Mackay since 'the start of the year'.

"Where is the bank loot now, Darren?"

"I think Raymond Adam has it." Darren replied. "You looking for a car loan?"

"No. Just thirty bob." Fleming said with a smile.

On Saturday morning Fleming went to Lauradale at his suggested time of ten o'clock. He parked next to the black and red Mini Cooper that he guessed belonged to Lorna Mackay.

He was greeted at the door by Laura Mackay who showed him through to the large front lounge, whispering to him on the way, that Gregor was still in Aberdeen. Lorna Mackay was seated on the leather settee to the left and rose as her mother and Fleming came into the room. Her mother's introductions were an unnecessary etiquette. Lorna was very similar to the black and white snapshot of her mother. Fleming was invited to sit beside Lorna on the settee. While he had no objections, he felt that Mrs Mackay was engaging in stage management.

Laura Mackay excused herself as she expected that the conversation might progress more easily without her. True though that was, Fleming considered this move to be out of character for Laura Mackay.

He asked Lorna to tell him what she was studying at university and how her exam had gone in January. As the girl began to reply, Fleming rose slowly from the settee and went round to the wall table behind the couch. He put a finger to his own lips to suggest that she make no remark concerning his actions, but her voice had slowed down as she looked at him. Her eyes were asking 'what are you doing?' Fleming gestured to her to keep talking. Looking behind a photograph frame on the table he saw a small device showing a red power button. He went back to the settee and returned the chat on Lorna's degree course. He worried that Laura Mackay might appear with a tray and teacups in order to ensure that they stayed where they were.

"Do these doors lead to the garden room?" Fleming asked Lorna, pointing to French doors at the end of the lounge.

"Yes, they do." Lorna replied. "Would you like to see it?"

"I would indeed." Fleming told her, rising again. "Gordon Macrae has told me about it."

The garden room was certainly impressive and, as far as Fleming could tell, it was free from recording devices.

"I have been admiring your gold earrings." Fleming remarked, now that they were away from the listening device. "I think they call that a teardrop design, don't they?"

"Yes, that's correct, Mr Fleming. Are you an authority on gold jewellery?" she asked mischievously.

"Only those that I recognise." Fleming said as if he did know a thing or two about jewellery. "Those earrings for example are part of a set and come with a matching pendant."

Lorna Mackay stopped and looked at him with a frightened look in her eyes. Fleming raised a hand to suggest there was no reason for her to be afraid.

"Were they a present from some kind soul?" he asked with a smile.

"As a matter of fact, they were." Lorna answered, looking guarded.

"The man who lived in the cottage has died. Did anyone tell you?" Fleming asked, purposefully watching Lorna's reaction to his first seven words. He saw what he expected, a tensing followed by relaxing but she was still uncertain of her ground.

"Yes, a terrible tragedy really. A heavy bookcase fell on him apparently."

"That's certainly true. Have you ever been in that cottage? I think that bookcase was always there." Fleming said casually.

"No, Mr Fleming. I have never been near the cottage."

"So, you would not have met the man who lived there, then?"

Lorna fell silent and her expression changed.

"Actually, I have met him." she said in a very quiet voice. "My parents would not approve, you see, but he spoke to me last summer when I was walking on the main road."

"What did he say?" Fleming asked, matching her quietness.

"He told me that I should never believe any bad thing that people said of him. It just wasn't true. I had no idea what he was talking about but it seemed to matter to him so I agreed. He said that he was a good man. He apologised for being late for my twenty-first birthday, which surprised me. How would he know about my twenty-first birthday, or even what age I was? He produced a small presentation box with two earrings and a pendant, just as you said. I told him that I would never use the pendant for I can't stand things round my neck, but I took the earrings. I told him they were lovely and thanked him. He seemed very pleased. I have no idea why he felt compelled to give me such a present. The man apparently never even speaks to other people. Now he is dead, poor man."

Fleming lifted his hand gingerly from his left jacket pocket. The pendant from the cottage rug hung from his fingers.

"That's the one. You have got it." Lorna breathed excitedly.

"Yes, my dear and if you had gone to the cottage you would have found this on the second top shelf of the bookcase. Here, take it, he would have wanted you to have it."

Lorna took the pendant carefully and mouthed the words 'Thank you'.

"Now, on a different topic," Fleming said assertively but quietly. "Can you remember the date when you and your dad flew back from Florida?" he asked with no hint of the gamble he felt he was taking.

"Yes, I do. It was the sixth of January. Cutting it fine, really. I started back at uni. the next day."

"Where do you stay, Lorna, in Aberdeen? Are there student rooms or what?"

"I share a flat with two other girls, Mr Fleming. Dad owns the flat actually."

"Oh I see." Fleming laughed. "That's handy. But your dad never stays there, even temporarily?"

"No. The company has a couple of 'guest flats' in Aberdeen. So he is never usually stuck for temporary accommodation. He will be in one of them this weekend, I would imagine."

"Do you and your dad meet up much in Aberdeen when you are both there?" Fleming asked, expecting a positive answer.

"No, not really. Different age groups and interests, you see. He told me in January not to come looking for him unless it was an emergency for he was going to be really busy. He told me not to go to my grandparent's house either. He wanted me to study hard when I had the chance."

"Did you see him after the exams?"

"Yes. The day after the exams he came to pick me up and take me out for dinner because I thought I had done well in my papers."

"He's pretty good to you, your dad, is he not?" Fleming said easily.

"Yes. He's always supported me and protected me. It can be embarrassing at times."

"Really? How can that be embarrassing?" Fleming asked, aware of his own feelings towards his children.

"Well, take the man at the cottage for instance. My dad told me not to take anything to do with him. 'You don't know where he's been'. He made the poor man sound like a dirty handkerchief or something." Lorna said with obvious opposition to her father's attitude.

"When was this advice given, recently?"

"Eh yes. I think it was when we were coming back from Florida. He is a bit too controlling, my dad. There is just far too much time on these transatlantic flights for parental guidance on any subject. When he got to the sex education bit I just told him to can it. The old ladies behind us were far too interested." she said, smiling and developing dimples on her cheeks.

Fleming laughed. They began to walk back to the lounge, still talking idly on the subject of air travel. Laura

Mackay was standing in the doorway from the hall trying her best to look pleasant.

"Oh, Mrs Mackay." said Fleming in an upbeat tone. "Would you believe that I found my nurse from Newton Mearns, thanks entirely to you?"

"That's remarkable, Mr Fleming. How is her mother?"

"Doing well actually, but she was going to the Royal Infirmary for surgery. I will phone Alison later in the week to hear how things went."

The weekend passed without too much to interest Fleming on the subject of the late George Prentice. Douglas Campbell had told him that the Procurator Fiscal had been in touch with Raymond Adam over the Prentice case. Mrs Rankine was keen to make funeral arrangements and had learned that a local Corran Bay funeral would be cheaper than transporting her brother back to Falkirk for cremation. Following Raymond Adam's pessimistic prognosis of the enquiry, the Procurator Fiscal had released the body for burial. Campbell had known nothing of this until Raymond Adam had called him to ask that Campbell attend the funeral on behalf of the police. Campbell asked Fleming if he would accompany him. Fleming had agreed.

He called in at Lauradale on Sunday afternoon to inform Laura Mackay and Gordon Macrae of the funeral arrangements.

When Tuesday came the attendance was as small as Fleming expected. He and Douglas Campbell were joined

on the front pews by Mrs Rankine, Gordon Macrae and
Lorna Mackay. A middle aged gentle man came in late
and sat at the back.

The clergyman paused as he noticed the small
congregation but this had happened before. He carried on,
pretending not to have noticed.

The service was brief and quietly spoken. There was no
need to raise his voice for the sake of one man. The eulogy
was written from the reports given to him by an unforgiving
sister but paraphrased euphemistically by a more forgiving
minister. Seeking forgiveness and understanding for sins
that George Prentice had undeniably been guilty of, was
the main theme. When the organist had drowned out the
singing of the twenty-third psalm, all left for the cemetery.
As the group shuffled around the grave trying to find a
remote place within respectful distance, Fleming noticed
that Lorna Mackay was wearing her gold earrings, the
ones Prentice had given her. She was also wearing the
pendant. Fleming wanted to mention this but the girl was
showing some emotion and he decided against any
approach.

To Fleming's right, at a respectable distance, council
workers waited to complete the lowering of the coffin and
subsequent interment. As the minister called for prayer,
Fleming noticed a figure in black behind the workmen, it
was Mrs Mackay. After the prayer she was walking
towards the cemetery gates. He looked across at Lorna
Mackay who looked in the direction to which he had been

looking. She obviously saw and recognised her mother. Her face looked solemn.

Mrs Rankine thanked the clergyman and then moved to each of the others in turn, thanking them for attending. She knew none of them. Fleming introduced himself and told her of the others present.

"I never thought that my brother actually knew this many people." she said. It seemed like a joke but nobody laughed. "I expected to be on my own here."

"My wife would have come too, Mrs Rankine, but she is not keeping well at the moment." It was Gordon Macrae who spoke, his darting eyes suggesting that his explanation was not for Mrs Rankine alone, but the others as well.

"It is such a pity that we were not given the time to know your brother better." Lorna Mackay said with genuine affection.

"Oh, that is not something for a lovely girl like you to worry about." Mrs Rankine replied showing that her own feelings towards her brother had not lightened much following his death.

"I am beginning to understand your brother a little better, Mrs Rankine. I wonder if he was ever as black as you would have him painted." Fleming said with a smile.

"What do you mean, Mr Fleming?"

"I will be happy to elaborate when I am in a better position to do so, Mrs Rankine. In the meantime, remember your brother as you knew him, not as others have portrayed him."

Mrs Rankine looked to her left to find Lorna Mackay and Gordon Macrae nodding in agreement.

"I will try, Mr Fleming. Thank you."

Mrs Rankine returned to the clergyman who had waited to speak to her again. Lorna Mackay waited beside the grave while the others made their way slowly towards the cemetery gates and the car park.

"What was all that about Prentice not being as bad as he's painted?" Campbell asked Fleming when nobody else was in earshot.

"She has always accepted without question that her brother had done everything he was accused of. For that reason she has harboured a hatred for him since, not based on any facts, just the shame brought to the family by his conviction." Fleming explained.

"That's understandable." Campbell replied.

"Only if you believe everything you read." Fleming said sardonically.

As they passed the gates Fleming recognised the tall, dark-haired man standing outside the entrance to the car park; the man previously occupying the rearmost pew of the church.

"Mr Scott." Fleming said in acknowledgement as he and Campbell walked past. The man stood open-mouthed as the two policemen carried on into the car park.

"Who was that?" Campbell asked.

"Some sort of Probation Officer." Fleming told him, making him no wiser. When they reached their car Fleming asked Campbell to stay outside the vehicle.

"Are we not leaving?" Campbell asked, revealing how pleased he was that this business was over.

"I want to see how long it takes young Lorna to leave that graveside." he said, again leaving Campbell perplexed, totally perplexed.

Lorna Mackay emerged from the cemetery a few paces behind the minister and Mrs Rankine. She was walking with her head down, deep in thought and not seeming to want company.

When Mrs Rankine approached her car, Fleming asked her, "Did you recognise Mr Scott?"

Mrs Rankine turned and stared back at the man Fleming had supposed was Scott. He was boarding his own car now.

"Yes, that's right. I knew I had seen him before."

Fleming had taken out a notepad from his pocket to note the registration number of Mr Scott's car. Mrs Rankine was looking at the notepad and it made Fleming smile.

"I am not forgetting about George's aborted letter, Mrs Rankine. I will send it to you, never fear."

When he looked back towards the dark blue car it was already out on the road and the registration plate was no longer visible.

Lorna Mackay was standing beside her Mini Cooper, leaning pensively on the roof and staring back towards the cemetery.

"Give me a second here, Dougie." Fleming said, walking over to her.

"Did you notice your mum?" he said softly.

Lorna turned slowly to face him.

"Why? Why did she come here when she had said that she wouldn't? She could have come with me if she wanted, but instead she just appears and disappears. What was that about?"

"Maybe someday she will choose to explain everything to you, Lorna. In the meantime, she obviously prefers to keep her answers to herself. It might be better not to mention to her that you saw her there. I also suspect that it would be unwise to mention it to your dad."

"No. I won't be doing that." she agreed.

"You wore his pendant for him. That was good of you." Fleming remarked.

"It was good of him too, Mr Fleming." Lorna said as if tormented by questions that occurred to her.

"See you later" Fleming told her and turned to walk back towards Campbell.

As he was unlocking the car a tearful Lorna came towards him and pressed a coin into his hand. Fleming looked down at the single one pence coin.

"What's this, Lorna?"

"The one that has finally dropped, Mr Fleming." she said through her tears. She turned around promptly and went to her car. In no time at all the little Mini was out of the car park and speeding along the road.

"What's up with her?" Campbell asked.

"Just a family thing, Dougie. I never expected that girl to cry over anything but there you are."

EIGHT

"What possible good would it do?" Raymond Adam said heatedly. "The man is dead and buried now."

"He didn't die of natural causes though, did he? And whoever killed him probably had the same misconception as everyone else." Fleming reasoned. "The murder of Laura Purdie led to a suspect conviction at best."

"There is nothing to justify an interrogation of Mrs Macrae on the subject of her daughter's death." the Detective Chief Inspector said as if to end the matter.

"I'm afraid there is." Fleming said firmly. "But we can't discuss it over the phone."

"Sounds like you want me back up there." Raymond Adam said with a heavy, exasperated sigh. He hated leaving his home patch but the unresolved death of George Prentice did bother him and Fleming could be the man to open things up. "You better be right about this, Fleming."

Andrew Fleming could not be sure that he was right about anything but he did believe what Alison Swarbeck had told him. What she had told him and nobody else until now. Before calling Raymond Adam he had called

Alison and enquired about her mother's condition and her own readiness to speak to a detective chief inspector. She might have to confirm her full account before going back home to New York.

"Yes sir, we need to talk. If you still have that pre-decimal cash with you, could you bring up a £1 note and a 10/- note please."

"Your dad will be home tomorrow, can you not wait another day?" Laura Mackay pleaded.

"No Mum, I am due back and I need all the class time I can get this year. Dad would be the first to tell me that." her daughter insisted as she folded her clean clothing and placed it in her sports bag.

"I don't suppose you have seen your Gran and Papa Turnbull for a while. You haven't been there since you came back in January, have you?"

"No, Mum, but I did have an exam to prepare for then. I hope to visit them this incoming week, though. I still have presents for them." Lorna said a little more cheerfully. "Dad took me out for dinner after my exam and told me that they were both fine."

"How did he know? Had he been to see them?" Laura Mackay asked with some surprise. "He never told me about it. It's not like him to visit my parents on his own. I usually have to bribe him, or drag him kicking and screaming."

"Oh Mum, really. He never actually said that he had

been there to visit them. Maybe he was just assuming that they were okay after you spoke to them at Christmas. If they were all right at Christmas then they were all right in January. I'll let you know how I find them next week." Lorna promised.

The two cars sat side-by-side on the machair by the shore road, both facing the sea. Fleming had joined Raymond Adam in his car.

Andrew Fleming had brought with him his folder of copy press cuttings concerning the George Purdie murder and rape trial. He used them to give Adam an overview of the circumstances that were reported in evidence to the court.

"It is obvious from these accounts," Fleming said, tapping the folder, "that no cross examination took place in respect of the two leading witnesses, the girl's mother and the girl's fifteen year old friend, Alison Henderson, now Swarbeck. Easy to understand when you are defending George Prentice and the dead girl's mother is distraught at the death of her daughter. The young friend is an innocent fifteen year old in awe of her court surroundings and also emotionally affected by the death. Bear in mind that the defence counsel had been provided with no alternative version of events with which to combat the prosecution case. George Prentice was stubbornly silent to both sides of this case.

Raymond Adam was listening intently.

"The main thrust of the prosecution case was the involvement on that one particular day of George Prentice and Laura Purdie. Witnesses saw them together at the fairground. The only witness to see George Prentice afterwards saw him alone, as he came running from the woods, out of breath. When the body was found in the woods, a week later, there was a cigarette lighter lying nearby with the initials GP engraved on it."

"George Prentice." Adam said, acknowledging the supposed significance.

"Yes, the prosecution said so too and nobody argued otherwise. The man in charge of the 'Waltzer' machine identified the lighter as being of the same type as the one being used by the girl to light cigarettes for both her and Prentice." Fleming explained. "Now I know from a very grown-up Alison Henderson that Laura Purdie had been in possession of that lighter before she met George Prentice. Like the cigarettes and the money, that lighter had been stolen from her mother, Griselda Purdie."

"Griselda Purdie? As in Elda Macrae?" Adam asked with amazement. "So, the letters GP could have stood equally well for her own mother. Why did Jock Cameron not see that?"

"Well, a couple of reasons, sir. The girl's mother was universally known, and made herself known, as Elda Purdie. Only on official documents and her daughter's headstone in Linn Cemetery, does the full and proper name of her mother appear. To you, me, Jock Cameron and even Gordon Macrae, she is Elda. The other reason is that Jock Cameron did not have the evidence of Alison Henderson. The young girl was never going to volunteer answers to unasked questions. It was a problem back then and it's still a problem today."

"So this coincidence with the initials, should it change the verdict?" Adam asked with a quizzical frown.

"Only when you hear what else Alison Henderson or Swarbeck had to say. She places Griselda Purdie at the fairground on the day of her daughter's disappearance. The woman was drunk and angry, really angry. Elda was searching for the daughter who had stolen her lighter, her fags, her money and had used her make-up. For your own convenience, Chief Inspector, I have typed out the statement that I took from Alison Swarbeck. It gives her telephone number at her parents' home. Her mother has been ill, so I waited for improvement there before raising this with you."

Raymond Adam looked at Fleming in disbelief as he took the typed document.

"So this enquiry had to wait for her mother to get better?"

"This enquiry was not in the best of health either, Chief Inspector. My compassion is ubiquitous." Fleming said soberly.

Adam began to read the statement he had been handed. When he had finished he folded the paper and placed it in his inside pocket.

"All right, so we speak to Mrs Macrae but only on her failure to disclose her presence at the fairground and her ownership of the lighter."

Fleming felt cheated. He knew that Raymond Adam would not want to be the one to bring out the inadequacies of a High Court trial and its preceding investigation by the CID.

She can tell us things about this case that have lain hidden for years." Fleming said confidently.

"Right, I'm going to the office to call this girl Swarbeck. It is in both our interests that I do that.

"Of course." said Fleming. "New evidence is simply that. Nobody is looking for heads to roll on the basis of the previously unknown."

"I must confirm this 'new evidence' of yours before I go near the Macraes."

Fleming parked outside the police office and waited for Raymond Adam. Twenty five minutes later the Detective Chief Inspector emerged from the office and waved to Fleming to join him in his CID car. Alison Swarbeck had confirmed her statement it seemed.

When Raymond Adam and Andrew Fleming arrived at the cottage in Lauradale Estate they were met at the door by Gordon Macrae. He showed a brief hint of annoyance but invited them in.

"We have come to speak with Mrs Macrae, if that is possible." Adam said hopefully, having found the lounge to be empty.

"She is in her bed, Chief Inspector. Her health is poorer than when you saw her last." Macrae said as he moved towards the door.

The officers heard him speak to his wife from her bedroom door.

"Ah, you are awake, Elda. The police are here to speak to you again. It's Detective Chief Inspector Adam and Constable Fleming."

"Let them come in, Gordon. I can't get up, dear." she answered in a quiet, breathless voice.

Gordon Macrae asked the officers to see his wife in her bed and opened the bedroom door wide for them. Elda was wearing a dressing gown in bed but Fleming could immediately see that the woman was thinner and older looking. She had lost colour and did not look well.

Raymond Adam edged closer to the side of the bed and apologised to Mrs Macrae for having to return to speak to her again on the death of her daughter in 1963. She stared back at him, silent and solemn.

"We know some things now that we did not know back then, Mrs Macrae." he began. "We know that on the day that Laura disappeared, you visited the fairground yourself. You were angry and under the influence of drink."

Elda Macrae continued to stare back at him without response or change of expression. She had done nothing to react.

"We are told that you were angry with your daughter

and were trying to find her." Adam continued, his caution making him appear clumsy and awkward.

"Why would I be angry at my daughter?" Elda Macrae asked in a rasping, defiant whisper.

Fleming stepped closer to the bed, pulling items from his pocket as he did so. He flung them onto the bedcover. Elda Macrae looked down at a brass lighter with GP engraved on it, a twenty pack of Embassy tipped cigarettes, a £1 note, a 10/- note and a pair of tights. A short painful cry issued from Elda's mouth and her head fell forward to be met by her rising, quivering hands. Behind these hands she began to sob.

Fleming was aware of the cold stares of objection from Raymond Adam and Gordon Macrae but kept watching the old woman.

"She stole them from me." Elda protested without removing her hands from her face. "She was always stealing from me and then ..." she broke off to shake her head from side to side behind her hands as if recalling a painful memory.

"What else did she do, Mrs Macrae?" Fleming asked in a quiet, sympathetic voice. "How else did she let you down?"

There was no immediate answer, just more sobbing. Fleming watched and waited, making Raymond Adam and Gordon Macrae follow suit.

"She just lay there ... with that Prentice on top of her. She wasn't fighting him off. She wasn't struggling with him. He didn't rape her."

Her voice was trembling but remained clear and distinct. Her hands remained over her face, providing anonymity, so that her confession felt like it was for her own consumption. Realising what she had just said, she lowered her hands and kept her head bowed.

"He didn't rape her and he never killed her." she said in a resigned voice, little more than a whisper.

"We know, Mrs Macrae, we know." Fleming told in the same quiet, sympathetic tone as before. "What really happened? Do you remember?"

Still staring blindly at her bedcover, Elda Macrae was calm as she spoke.

"I found the pair of them in that wood. I yelled when I realised it was Laura. He ran away. Laura was still lying there when I reached her. I just dropped down on top of her with my knees and started battering her. She fought back like she had done before but I gripped her round the neck. I squeezed and kept squeezing until she stopped fighting back. These things ..." she pointed at the items on the bed. "These things were in her pockets. She was wearing my make-up.

"Did you realise how far you had gone?" Fleming asked with sympathetic concern.

"Not right away." Elda Macrae said sadly, back to staring at the bedcover. Her eyes just stared back at me as if she couldn't believe what her own mother had just done to her. As you say, I was drunk, but I still knew that Laura was dead. I screamed in fright and her wee face ..." Elda began to sob again. "I turned her over so she couldn't look at me anymore."

Gordon Macrae moved around Raymond Adam to place a supporting arm round Elda's shoulders.

"Oh Elda dear, what have you done? What a heavy sin to be carrying all these years."

"I am sorry, Gordon. I've really let you down." she whimpered, her hand finding his on top of the bed.

Fleming lifted away the lighter, cigarettes and tights, returning them to his pockets. Raymond Adam lifted the old bank notes. The police officers allowed the Macraes to settle.

"What happens now, Chief Inspector?" Gordon Macrae asked.

"We must set the record straight, Mr Macrae. I will charge Mrs Macrae with the murder of her daughter in 1963 and report the new circumstances to the Procurator Fiscal. After that he makes the decisions. Who is your wife's doctor?"

Elda Macrae looked up for the first time and told Adam who her doctor was before smiling at her husband. It was a forced smile, simply reflecting the gratitude she was due to Gordon.

"It's all right, Gordon."

Raymond Adam and Andrew Fleming took out their notebooks and Raymond Adam formally charged her with murder of her daughter as he had said he would.

"I will consult with your doctor but I can see that you

are in no condition to be placed in custody. What is your current state of health, Mrs Macrae?"

The Macraes looked at each other.

"Gordon, bring me over my handbag, please." Elda asked.

When she was given her handbag she opened it and took out a white appointment card which she handed to her husband. The big highlander, the strength of her life, looked at the card and his head fell into a mighty hand with a sad, "Oh no, Dear God."

Raymond Adam bent over to read what he could of the card in Macrae's other hand and saw only the words 'Oncology Outpatients'. He looked at the frail figure in the bed whose eyes showed concern, but not for herself. Adam looked across at Fleming and shook his head gently, his expression grim. Nothing had been said but nothing needed to be said.

Raymond Adam rose and spoke softly into Gordon Macrae's ear. Gordon's face was still hidden in his hand.

"We will go now and leave you good folks in peace. I am so sorry."

The two police officers returned to their vehicle without speaking. As he drove away, Raymond Adam asked Fleming, "You proud of that stunt you pulled back there?"

"Not at the moment." was Fleming's reply.

As they approached the junction of the estate road with the smaller road leading to and from the empty cottage, a blue car sped out in front of them forcing Adam to brake. Fleming noted the registration number.

"Did you get a look at that guy?" Adam asked.

"Dark hair, dark jacket, that's about all, but I did get the car number." Fleming told him, writing the number in his notebook.

"I think we should check the cottage." Adam said. "We could never hope to catch that character."

Fleming knew what he meant – he (Adam) could never hope to catch that character. DCIs don't race and chase.

The cottage was not damaged but a window at the rear had been entered. The window and the frame had previously been painted in white gloss paint without opening the window to do the job. The paint that had bridged the seams around the window had broken and was now sharp and jagged as a result of the sash being forced upwards.

"That guy was in here." Fleming concluded, squinting at the paintwork for any indication of prints.

"You don't have your kit with you, sir?" Fleming said boldly. "So let's see what else we can find."

He climbed through the open window, pointing out to Adam the mud on the inner window shelf. Raymond Adam would not be following him that was certain. It just wasn't possible.

"What are you hoping to find?" Adam called in to him.

"You would really have to ask the guy before me." Fleming answered. "He presumably knew."

Fleming checked the rooms quickly, aware of Adams impatience as he waited outside. The front door had a heavy box lock and could not be opened. Fleming touched nothing. His attention was drawn to the bookcase. He had personally returned all the books, with Hamish MacLeod and turned each book over to flick the pages in order to reveal any document hidden inside the pages. There was now a single book in a double space, leaning at an angle against the next hard cover. Another book, presumably the one removed, now lay horizontally across the tops of the books on that shelf. Fleming just knew that he had not left them like this.

Using his handkerchief, he lifted the flat book away but his grip of it was not secure. He managed to read that it was a copy of 'Lorna Doone' by R.D. Blackmore, before the book fell to the floor. When it landed, the book fell open and exposed a letter jammed in the spine. The letter was addressed to George Prentice at Barlinnie Prison, Glasgow. The postage stamp had cost 3d. The date stamp was for July 1964.

Fleming was now convinced that someone had inserted this letter into the book after Fleming's last visit to the cottage, perhaps significantly, after the murder of George Prentice.

Using his handkerchief again, Fleming carried the book and letter to the rear window. Raymond Adam was looking at a small patch of garden nearby. He noticed Fleming's return and came to the window.

"Somebody's been digging there." he commented. "Did you find anything?"

"Yes, I did." Fleming said, and explained the book he was holding. "I suppose our intruder broke in just to replace this letter, so these things will have to be examined for fingerprints."

Raymond Adam looked back towards the garden ground briefly before going to his car for a brown paper bag. He told Fleming to drop the book and letter into the bag. He took the bag to the car as Fleming climbed out of the window. The Chief Inspector came back and looked around until he found a shovel with fresh mud on the blade. He took the shovel over to the garden.

"He never dug very deep with this thing. It should be easy to check out."

Adam began to dig at the loosened soil and it soon became apparent that there was nothing to find. Fleming considered that the letter may have been buried in the garden until it seemed safe to recover and replace it. He went to the dustbin at the corner of the building. The bin contained empty packets and tins but on top of these was a plastic food container with an airtight lid. The outside of the container was dirty with soil. Fleming lifted it out carefully and handed it to the DCI.

"Good man." Adam said. "I think you are right about this being hidden in the garden. I'll get Dougie Campbell and Darren Black to collect a key and go over this cottage again. The book, the letter and that thing you just found, I'll deal with myself."

Now Fleming felt cheated. He would dearly love to know what that letter said but he might never see it again.

On their return to the police office, Raymond Adam instructed Campbell and Black on what he wanted done at the cottage. Fleming noticed that he never told them anything about the Macrae interview.

"Now Andrew, let's see what Charlie can give us on that car number."

The blue car seen rushing away from the cottage was registered to A.P.I. Ltd. at an industrial estate in Aberdeen.

"Sounds like one of these damned oil businesses." Adam said, sounding exasperated. "Get me a phone number for them, Charlie."

Charlie Macdonald duly obliged.

Raymond Adam took Fleming back to the CID room where they now had the room to themselves. He used the telephone to call the Aberdeen number. When his call was answered, he asked, "What exactly is it that you people do?"

His expression and tone softened a little.

"Oh, I wasn't expecting that," he told the other party. "I'm sorry."

"Private Investigators." he said to Fleming. "We can't really deal with this by speaking to these people on the telephone. Private investigators are not allowed to break into cottages. I just might have to go to Aberdeen over this one. You would want to come, I know that, Andrew, but procedure dictates that I take someone like Dougie with me. You deserve it but you can't come with me, I just want you to know that."

"Thank you, sir. I appreciate that but what I would like, is to see that letter once it has been scanned for prints."

Adam thought about it. The letter would probably become a court production.

"I'll make you a copy. How's that? For a guy that would type out a statement for me, it's the least I can do. Before we get ahead of ourselves here, maybe we should be sure that the envelope actually contains a letter."

Fleming followed the big man out to his car where Adam donned a pair of spectacles and latex gloves. From his breast pocket he took out a pair of tweezers. On the back seat of his car he spilled the book from the paper bag before holding it up by the ends of the spine, allowing the envelope to fall out. Using the tweezers he pulled the single page of writing from the envelope and unfolded it. The letter had come from Aberdeen and read;

"Dear George, I am so sorry for you and what has happened. I do not believe that someone as kind and gentle as you could ever attack and kill a girl. I don't care what the world thinks of you, George, I know you are innocent. You will be in jail for a long time and life will not be good for you. I just want you to know that we have a lovely little girl and her name is Lorna. Don't tell anyone about us George and don't write back. My father would only burn any letters you sent so I am not telling you my address. Life will go on, George but we will never be together again. Your friend always, Laura X"

"You happy with that?" Adam asked. "Can I put it away now?"

"Yes, thanks, Chief Inspector." Fleming replied almost absent-mindedly.

"You're trying to figure this out already?" Adam asked in a critical tone but with a smile on his face.

"Actually the letter is not that surprising. It explains why George Prentice would be content to live in such poor conditions, despite his money, while pretending to be someone else. We know where he got the money and I had expected that he had killed the real Arthur Fraser to get it but I am not so sure about that now. What the letter doesn't explain is why a private investigator would benefit from visiting his home, especially after his death." Fleming said thoughtfully, as if to himself.

"Well, the PI won't be working for the department store or the insurers." Adam said confidently. "Our legal boffins are still trying to figure out who is entitled to the return of the cash after all these years and in today's world. The ownership of the store has changed several times and so has the original insurance company. Sending a PI to Lauradale would do nothing to sort that out."

"No, and they would not use a PI from Aberdeen, anyway, would they? Wonder who the client is though?" Fleming asked foxily.

Raymond Adam smiled.

"I'll let you know." he said in a 'be patient' sort of tone as he climbed into the car and started the engine. He lowered the window and grinned at Fleming before driving away.

"Don't forget to put your tights back on."

Fleming smiled and rejected the thought of replying by digit.

Gregor Mackay was still too busy to come home and Laura had known many times like these. When she had stayed in Aberdeen she had gone to the shops, or to her parents, or both, but here her loneliness was palpable. She had not seen Elda Macrae in ages and it always seemed to be Gordon on his own in the car when it passed the front of her house. She recalled how Elda had not attended George Prentice's funeral because she had been unwell. She knew what Elda thought of George, even if she only knew him as Arthur Fraser. Why would she attend the funeral of a man who was alleged to have killed her daughter? Elda had every reason to hate George on the basis of what she now knew.

With a bunch of daffodils from her own garden, Laura set off walking up to the Macraes' cottage.

Gordon Macrae was his usual friendly, welcoming self

and invited Laura in to the lounge. Elda was sitting there in her dressing gown.

"How are you keeping, my dear?" Laura asked with sincere interest. "I hear that you were not too well."

"I wasn't very good, that's true." Elda said quietly. "I have been to the hospital and they checked me for cancer. They took X-rays and never saw anything obvious. They took blood and apparently I am short of iron and my platelets are low, whatever that means. So I have tablets."

"Are they doing you any good?" Laura asked.

"They seem to be helping. I wouldn't be up out of bed before, too weak, you see. Now I can manage to walk about indoors and sit if I get tired. I am not ready to go out yet."

"So you are doing all the cooking and shopping, Gordon?" Laura asked with mock sympathy. "If I can help in any way just let me know. I'm bouncing about in that big house like a pea in a drum. I could help you anytime you want. Do you like things like liver, foie gras, herbs, spinach, kidney beans? These have iron, don't they? Even chocolate, Elda, there is iron in cocoa, you know.

"I don't mind any of these things, Laura, but I have no appetite. I only want tiny amounts of anything that I am eating. I am losing interest really."

"Are you depressed, Elda? That is quite a different thing to your blood issues." Laura asked, moving closer to her friend.

"I have been depressed before." Elda said as if depression was no big deal. "Gordon was always the best medicine for my depression."

"Well, Gordon is still here Elda and he is probably still your best medicine."

Elda smiled and looked at Gordon before turning back to Laura.

"I had the police back again, you know." she began.

"No, Elda." Gordon pleaded. He obviously did not want the matter raised. Laura said nothing to prompt either of them.

"Neither of us is getting any younger, Gordon and me. I have been hiding a terrible secret for twenty-two years, something I never even told Gordon about. The other day the police came to me and spoke about it. I have been charged with the murder of my own daughter in 1963. Gordon wasn't by my side back then. I could have used him then but all I had was drink. I strangled my own daughter Laura and that poor man over the back here served eighteen years for my crime."

She stopped and began to cry. She took a paper handkerchief from her pocket to wipe her eyes.

Laura Mackay sat opposite her, open-mouthed and silent. She rose to her feet and left the daffodils in her chair as she made for the door. Without a word being uttered she left the cottage and went home. Well before reaching her home Laura Mackay was weeping uncontrollably.

Raymond Adam had called the Grampian Police out of courtesy and informed them of an enquiry that he wished to conduct personally at the premises of A.P.I. Ltd.

Accompanied by Douglas Campbell he now sat opposite the business unit looking at the parked cars.

"Don't see that same car here, Dougie. Let's go in."

Behind a sliding glass panel window the receptionist looked at the two visitors as if she already knew their profession.

"Can I help you?" the words sounded mechanical.

"We are both CID officers. Is there someone here we can speak to about a dark blue car that this company owns?" Adam said formally.

"Sure." She turned and nodded a summons to some-body at the other end of the open plan room. She walked towards the man as he approached and whispered to him as he passed her.

"Gentlemen, I am Henry Dobson, what can I do to help you?" the tall, dark haired man asked.

Raymond Adam and Douglas Campbell introduced themselves and presented their warrant cards for Dobson to see.

"I would like to speak to the man who was using this car two days ago near an estate cottage on the west coast." Adam said as he passed between the glass panels a piece of paper with the description and registration number of the car.

"We don't work the west coast, are you sure you've got the number right?" Dobson asked, aware that the car represented by the number was not outside.

"The number is correct." Adam said firmly. "It is registered to this company, isn't it?"

Now Dobson lowered his gaze and studied the piece of paper as if trying to place the vehicle.

"I think that could be the Ford that Gibson uses, Colin Gibson. He's not in today." Dobson said unhelpfully.

"Mr Dobson, I did not come all this way to be told that this man is day off. We are here in relation to a serious crime investigation so if you feel above suspicion then sort out the attitude problem and cooperate."

"Okay, fair enough." Dobson said cheekily. "Colin Gibson has been working on something for one of the oil bosses here in Aberdeen, not all the time, but on and off for some time. I don't know exactly what he is doing but it is not a murder or anything. I think he was trying to trace somebody for the guy but I don't have details."

Dobson then wrote on the same piece of paper that Adam had given him and returned it to him.

"That is Colin Gibson's address but he might not be home 'til late. Failing that he is due to be in here tomorrow morning at eight-thirty."

Behind his back, the receptionist was staring at Dobson in disbelief.

"Thank you, Mr Dobson. Your cooperation is appreciated."

Dobson merely nodded in response, his eyes distinctly unfriendly.

Adam and Campbell returned to their car but Raymond Adam paused for a moment to note the registration numbers of all vehicles parked in front of and adjacent to the premises of A.P.I. Ltd. He didn't care that he was being watched as he did so. Campbell studied the street map of Aberdeen to find Gibson's address.

Half an hour later the pair were parked outside the address, a smart 1970's bungalow. The surrounding houses were of similar appearance and construction. The two police officers wondered what these houses were worth in the oil-rich days for Aberdeen.

"What do you suppose a Private Eye earns here, Dougie?"

"Obviously more than you might expect him to." was Campbell's reply.

"Let's see if anyone is at home." Adam suggested as he opened his door and hauled himself upwards.

The pair stood at the house door, having rung the bell twice and having seen the 'Gibson' nameplate.

"I'm not happy with this." Adam said with typical frustration and impatience. "I'm going to knock a few doors."

He went directly across the street to a house that overlooked the Gibson home. His knock on the door was answered by a portly lady in her sixties.

"Sorry to bother you but I wonder if you can confirm

for me that the house opposite is occupied by Colin Gibson? I believe he is a private investigator."

"A private investigator?" the woman looked shocked by the suggestion. "Colin works in the oil business, most of the people around here do."

"What kind of car does he drive?" Adams asked.

"A Mercedes. Ann, his wife, has one too."

"How long might it be before you could expect them to come home?" Adam asked, looking at his watch.

"They are not normally home until after eight o'clock at night." the woman said as if she took a pride in knowing such things.

"Thank you very much. You have been an immense help." Adam told her.

"Right Dougie, we are going back to that A.P.I. place. We seem to be getting the run-around here. Keep me right with my directions." Adam said as he slammed his car door and turned the ignition as if trying to break the key.

When they reached the office of A.P.I. Ltd. they found the premises closed and the vehicles gone.

"I do not believe this." Raymond Adam complained. "Would this crowd normally close at four o'clock, I wonder?"

Campbell gave his boss time to lower his blood pressure and then asked, "Where to, now?"

Raymond Adam took out his notebook and flicked backwards through the pages.

"Andy Fleming gave me an address – I said I would go

if I had time – ah, here it is, Brent Avenue, No. 22. See if you can find that, Dougie."

Campbell began to scour the index. "Who lives there?" he asked.

"The Turnbulls - Mrs Mackay's parents."

The Turnbulls were surprised to be receiving a visit from the CID officers and Raymond Adam apologised for the lack of warning, explaining how it had not actually been on their original agenda to be making this visit.

Once the initial confirmation of relationship between the Turnbulls and the Mackays had been established, Raymond Adam asked about the Turnbulls' knowledge of a man called George Prentice.

The older couple looked at each other and Mrs Turnbull shook her head as if she had no wish to answer. George Turnbull turned to face the Detective Chief Inspector.

"We know about him, what he is supposed to have done, what he went to prison for. That's what we know about him."

"I am surprised that you are as familiar with him as that." Raymond Adam said earnestly.

"Most people would have forgotten about the man. It seemed to strike a chord with both of you. Why was that?"

"Before he went to prison he was a friend of our daughter's." Mrs Turnbull said abruptly. "That's why we recognise the name."

"Do either of you recognise the name Arthur Fraser?" Adam asked without suggestion that they should.

"Only by name." George Turnbull said as if interested. "Gregor, our son-in-law, was intent in getting that man to leave. He was the one in the cottage at Lauradale," he turned to his wife as he continued, "the one who was always looking at Laura and Lorna."

She nodded.

"Did he ever do anything offensive with regard to your daughter and granddaughter?" Adam asked.

"Not that we know of, officer." George Turnbull replied. "The man had been there for two years and had bothered nobody. It was only in January that Gregor even mentioned the man."

"This January?" Douglas Campbell asked.

"It wasn't just Fraser he was interested in, was it George?" Mrs Turnbull said a little spitefully.

"No it wasn't. To let you understand, gentlemen, our son-in-law is normally far too busy, or unwilling, to come here on his own but in the second week in January he came here and told us that he would make sure that Fraser got out of Lauradale. Gregor was sure that the man was a criminal on the run or an ex-convict. He asked us if we knew of any ex-convicts who might be interested in our daughter."

"It was such a strange question for him to ask." Mrs Turnbull interjected. "It was only at Christmas, when I spoke to Laura on the telephone, that she confided in me that this Arthur Fraser reminded her of George Prentice. She had not told Gregor or Lorna, of course, and she was not prepared to say anything to her dad. Then suddenly, out of the blue, Gregor appears here in our home to ask a question like that."

"What did you tell him?" Adam asked with a smile of enjoyment at the story.

"We told him that we hoped there were no ex-convicts with an interest in our daughter. Why should there be?" George Turnbull said firmly. "But he wouldn't let it drop. Have you any old photographs? Any old press cuttings of killers or rapists? So it was quite obvious to us who he was getting at."

"We just told him that we don't consort with these kinds. We moved out of Glasgow to get away from them." Mrs Turnbull said, in much the same way that Adam could imagine her telling her son-in-law. "He seemed to settle down a bit after that. We never made him any the wiser."

"Is he easily made angry?" Raymond Adam asked.

"Very much so" George Turnbull replied. "When things are not suiting him he lets everybody know about it."

"Could he be violent?" Adam asked.

"I believe he could be," George Turnbull answered, "not that we have ever seen him behave that way."

"You are a former oil man, Mr Turnbull, do you know a man called Colin Gibson?" Adam asked without expectation.

"There are thousands of oil men as you put it, Chief Inspector, and I certainly don't know them all, but I do know one Colin Gibson. He is operating at a higher level than I ever did. I only know him because he is another executive in the same company as Gregor."

"Is he connected to a firm of private investigators? Does that seem likely, at all?"

"Not in any hands-on way, certainly not. I don't know what Colin has in the way of companies but he did provide funding for various small firms as part of an agreement with the local authority. A private investigations company may have been one for all I know."

"Colin Gibson runs about in a Mercedes?" Adam asked, looking for confirmation.

George Turnbull nodded.

"A new one every year."

"Have you spoken to your daughter, Laura, recently?" Adam asked inoffensively.

"Not for a day or two". Mrs Turnbull said. "But Lorna, our grand-daughter has called. She is coming round tomorrow."

"Of course, Lorna is at university here, I forgot." Adam said with a smile. "Did she know George Prentice at all?"

"Never." George Turnbull said firmly. "And she never will."

"These things are useful to know." Raymond Adam told him. "Do you suppose there is any way that Gregor overheard Laura talking to you on the telephone, or even heard from Laura directly, of how she suspected the presence of George Prentice in the form of Arthur Fraser?"

George Turnbull turned towards his wife.

"You are the one she spoke to. Was Gregor there when she was talking?"

"I am pretty sure he wasn't, at least, not as far as she knew. She specifically told me that she had no intention of telling him about George Prentice anyway. I can't imagine her saying that Fraser looked like him if there was any chance of Gregor overhearing."

"I see." said Adam. "So how did he find out?"

"What makes you think that he did?" George Turnbull asked.

"When they left for Florida, Gregor told the Macraes, Elda and Gordon, that he and Laura would be back in March. Gordon was house-watching for them, you see. Yet he comes back in early January with Lorna." Adam reasoned.

"Yes but that was work related." Mrs Turnbull objected.

"If he says so," said Raymond Adam, "but he is normally so busy that he cannot take time to visit you with Laura, yet he makes a surprise visit in the second week of January when Lorna is at university and Laura is in Florida and what does he choose to talk about?"

George Turnbull was looking thoughtful.

"I remember, back in 1982, I told Laura and Gregor

about seeing a man in our street who looked a lot like George Prentice. This guy just walked down the street without speaking to anyone but he spent time looking at us and our car. He had a long coat and small suitcase. I never knew George Prentice well enough to say that it was definitely him, but it somehow reminded me of him, just as this Fraser reminded Laura of him."

"But Gregor knew nothing about George Prentice." Mrs Turnbull said. "All we said was he had been a man who went to jail just before we had moved up to Aberdeen. Laura knew who we meant but he didn't."

"So he was given no reason to be interested in Prentice?" the Chief Inspector asked, needing to be clear that information on the past had not gone to Prentice from the family.

"No. None of us wanted him to ever know." George Turnbull insisted.

Raymond Adam looked back and forth between the Turnbulls considering how much he could afford to raise.

"A colleague of ours has spoken to the Macraes and to Laura and Lorna at different times and has been working quite successfully on the past issues that seem important to this case. He strongly suspects a connection between George Prentice and Lorna."

Mrs Turnbull gasped audibly.

"Is he correct?" Adam asked firmly. "This is not something to be repeated, it is another of these things that matter to us as we pursue our own interests. We are not out to destroy families or anything like that. We just need to make progress, to do that we need to understand the perspectives in order to see motive. George Prentice was murdered."

Again Mrs Turnbull gasped. George Turnbull looked puzzled.

"Our daughter said he had been killed by a falling bookcase, if it's that Arthur Fraser character you're speaking about."

"That was the first impression of his death, certainly, Mr Turnbull. No, he was killed. We know that now, what we don't yet know is by whom, or why."

"The man raped and killed a young girl, there must be people who would want to kill him." George Turnbull said simply, "Even if it happened a long time ago."

"Actually his guilt for these crimes is no longer as certain as it was thought to be back then. My question to you as grandparents is this, was George Prentice biologically related?"

Mrs Turnbull looked at the floor. George Turnbull squirmed in his chair, his hands twisting on his knees. He seemed to sense what Raymond Adam was sensing, that the question was being silently answered.

"Yes." George Turnbull blurted out, "But not a damn word of that to anyone. She would tell you," he said, pointing to his wife, who was now crying, "just how important it is for everyone's future. Lorna is Lorna Mackay, Gregor is her dad. The girl has lived her life without expecting to hear anything different."

"Like I said before, I have no intention of gossiping, Mr Turnbull." the Detective Chief Inspector said carefully, "But I must also consider matters as you believed them to be. Have either or both of you been to Lauradale Estate recently?"

Mrs Turnbull was shaking her head, unwilling to speak.

"We have only been there twice in the last ten years and not at all in the last five years. We see them when they come to us." George Turnbull said frankly.

"So, for the sake of straight recording neither of you killed George Prentice?" Adam said without suggesting otherwise.

"We would not have killed the man." Mrs Turnbull pleaded.

Her husband looked at her seriously before turning to Adam again.

"No, I suppose that is true. I could not do something like that, even to him."

"I am pleased to hear it." Raymond Adam said cheerfully, "In fact I will not be this pleased again until I know who did."

Fleming had called several times but Laura Mackay had not answered her telephone. It seemed unlike her to go away but if her car was gone, then so was she. He went to Lauradale to check for himself. Her car was parked in its usual spot and the covering of blown leaves suggested that it had stood for a day or two without going anywhere. There were no other cars present. Fleming went to the front door and rang the bell. After the second ring the door was opened reluctantly by Laura Mackay.

"Oh, Mr Fleming." she said as if he was the last person she had expected to see that morning. "Come in, come in."

"Have you been unwell?" Fleming asked.

"Not really." she said in a sad, hopeless voice. "Were you one of the people trying to call me?"

"Yes, I tried a few times. Then I got slightly concerned."

"Bless you, I just did not feel like speaking to anyone. For once I needed to be on my own."

Fleming noticed the cushions piled at one end of her settee and a travel rug folded at the other. He could imagine an undisturbed bed upstairs.

"So what has changed for you, Mrs Mackay? If you are not ill then you are certainly saddened. I haven't seen you before without a smile on your face."

This forced Laura Mackay to smile briefly.

"I haven't been outside in two days, Mr Fleming. Do you mind if we walk?"

"I have nothing against the idea at all, Mrs Mackay."

Laura Mackay put on a quilted jacket and locked the large front door behind them. She began to walk in the direction of the main road with Fleming watching her closely. Had she been eating? Was she strong enough for this?

"People always speak about skeletons in the cupboards, dark family secrets, unspoken memories and the sort of things that go with one to their grave. That sort of subject makes for good matinee movies or romantic novels, because then it is always some other anonymous person's experience. Do you understand what I mean, Mr Fleming?"

"Yes, I think I follow you." Fleming said easily.

"We can all live with our little secrets if we are allowed to, but then life can be turned upside down." She fell silent for several steps but Fleming did nothing to prompt her. "We could go along towards the cottage," she suggested as they neared the junction with the dirt road, "I haven't been along there since we moved here ten years ago. The cottage was in a terrible state then. I have no idea what Gregor did to improve it but it would take a lot of work before the letting agency was prepared to advertise it."

"How do you suppose George found it?" Fleming asked casually.

"If it was George, what makes you think it was the cottage he was looking for?" Laura Mackay asked, surprising Fleming.

"I see," said Fleming, "All right, how do you suppose he found you?"

"I don't know." she answered with an ironic laugh. "For a while I never realised he had. I didn't consider for a moment that Arthur Fraser could be anyone but Arthur Fraser from Glasgow, a complete stranger. He was untidy looking, hardly shaved, wore a hat unnecessarily and dressed in old clothes. He was everything that George Prentice was not and yet, there came a day when he was close enough for me to see. It must have been the way he was looking across at me or the way he turned to walk away but I suddenly thought about George. I had no suspicion that it actually was George Prentice, mind you. I only thought I had found someone similar. I even told my mother of how the man called Arthur Fraser was reminding me of George. I wouldn't dare to tell my dad, he could never understand."

"You only told your mother?" Fleming said in his 'is that so?' tone.

"Oh my goodness, yes, I was hardly going to tell Lorna that ..." her voice failed to compete what she might have said.

"Do you suppose George Prentice would feel the same way, about telling Lorna, I mean?" Fleming said sympathetically.

Laura Mackay stopped and looked at Fleming as if the thought had not occurred to her.

"She hasn't spoken to him."

"Yes, actually she has, but I do not think they discussed the matter of relationship. As you said earlier, some people are prepared to take secrets to their graves."

They walked on in silence. Laura Mackay was considering how typical it would be of George Prentice to take his knowledge of his beautiful student daughter to his grave. Fleming was considering that Laura Mackay had reacted late to the trauma of George Prentice's death, if that was all that troubled her.

As they were passing one of the trees nearest to the narrow road Fleming noticed broken fragments of a vehicle light lens in the long grass. There was a score in the bark of the tree. He lifted the pieces of coloured plastic and stuck them in his pocket. They looked fairly new and he recalled the speeding blue car that he had seen when he was with Raymond Adam.

He might have explained to Laura Mackay what he was doing but he found her staring across the undergrowth at the sunlit roof of the Macrae's cottage, lost in her own thoughts.

"How did you know about George being Lorna's father?" she asked without diverting her attention from the distant roof. "Did someone tell you?"

"You did, a few moments ago, before that it was simply a deduction."

"Based on what?" she asked without turning.

"Based on several unanswered questions about the man in the cottage; whether he was Arthur Fraser or someone else, why would he choose to come here to stay? Having come here to stay why would he be so defensive against the sociable approaches of other people, like the Macraes? Given that he was George Prentice, why would he show a peculiar interest in yourself and Lorna? Why, after eighteen years in prison without communication with his sister would he go to her and ask where the Turnbulls might have gone?"

Laura Mackay turned smartly. "He did?"

"Yes. Mrs Rankine could not tell him of course but I imagine that that did not stop him. As you said yourself, he was intent on finding you and he did. Having found you, he watched you and when Lorna came here, he watched her, secretly and silently satisfied to be close to you both. He never approached you, despite the temptation, am I right?"

She smiled and nodded. When she smiled it formed dimples in her cheeks, something Fleming had failed to notice before.

"He could probably guess at who Lorna was, but he actually spoke to her," Fleming continued. "Because a man would want to know what his daughter sounded like, how she spoke to people. Knowing who she was would not really be enough. He remembered her age, apparently. He gave her a belated twenty-first birthday present, did you know that?"

"No, I did not." Laura said with genuine surprise. "She never told me. Is that where the gold earrings came from?"

"It was indeed, so you see, I had more information than I needed to make my deduction." Fleming said confidently. He felt that the time was not right to mention the letter Laura had sent to Prentice in 1964.

"Poor George," Laura Mackay said sadly, "Look at this place. Even in the summertime this house will get none of the morning sunlight that the Macraes are getting.

It's hardly cosy living and Gregor refused him the chance to put heating in. George could have done that. He was a plumber, you know."

"Yes, I know. He was also an innocent man."

Laura Mackay's response was to break into tears. "I know, I know." she wept.

It was Fleming's turn to be surprised.

"How do you know, Mrs Mackay?"

"Because Elda killed her own daughter and never said a word to set George free. She told me herself." Laura was now crying steadily, wiping tears with her handkerchief. "That woman ruined my life and George's."

Fleming watched Laura Mackay as she alternately shook her head and wiped her eyes. Whoever had killed George Prentice, it was certainly not this lady.

"Do you want to see through the windows or will we just walk back?" he asked compassionately.

"We'll just go back." she said softly.

"Have we reached the bottom of what was troubling you?" Fleming asked hopefully.

"Yes, I suppose so. I don't know if I can ever forgive Elda Macrae." Laura Mackay said coldly.

"Her silence allowed her own life to progress." Fleming said evenly. "She never did anything in the knowledge that she was affecting you. She would tell you herself that Gordon Macrae has been the only worthwhile person in her life. She was holding on firmly to what she had. I wonder if anyone else would have been motivated to do otherwise." Fleming reflected. "As for Elda, she has not had the pleasure of having a daughter like Lorna, nor has she got the sort of health that you and I seem to enjoy."

Laura Mackay stopped and looked at Fleming. She smiled but said nothing before she began walking again.

"Gregor has been away a wee while." Fleming remarked.

"I am used to that Mr Fleming. Work comes first with Gregor, it always did. I can't really complain. I have been blessed in other ways. A good friend has reminded me of that."

She remained on the doorsteps to watch Fleming depart before unlocking her door and entering her home. The telephone was ringing and Laura Mackay answered it to find her husband on the line.

"Honey, where have you been? I've been trying for the last couple of days." Gregor Mackay sounded concerned.

"Haven't you got this lovely weather?" Laura asked cheerfully. "I've been out walking, Gregor. We have daffodils and crocuses everywhere."

"Are you out walking at night?" he asked sarcastically.

"No, but I was probably at the Macraes. Elda is quite ill apparently."

"Oh, I see." Gregor Mackay sounded almost apologetic. "Just as long as you are okay, honey. I should manage down in the next couple of days. Have the police been back bothering you?"

"No Gregor, I can honestly say they haven't been bothering me."

When Fleming reached the police office that afternoon, Douglas Campbell was waiting to tell him just how unsuccessful the search for the dark blue car had been.

"We ran back and forward across Aberdeen looking for this car but never found it yet." Campbell reported with a sneering tone in his voice.

"You should have tried the panel-beaters' workshops, Dougie." Fleming replied as he held up his cellophane bag of lens fragments.

"Where did you get these?"

"Beneath the tree the guy hit at Lauradale." Fleming said pleasantly. "Did you chaps learn anything at Aberdeen?"

"As a matter of fact we did." Campbell said triumphantly. "We learned who the biological father of Lorna Mackay is, or was."

"I could have told you that before you left, Dougie, but I imagine the big man has warned you not to talk about it, right?"

"There's nothing I can tell you, Fleming, you know it all."

"As a matter of fact I don't." said Fleming. "Did you get any unidentified fingerprints from the cottage?"

"Yes. We got three sets of prints, all the same person. One set on the handle of the poker and two on the bookcase, but like you say, we have no match. However by this time tomorrow you'll probably come in and tell me who they belong to." Campbell said cheekily.

"I am sorry, Elda, I truly am. I just thought about that poor man spending all that time in jail for something he didn't do." Laura Mackay explained. "I am too sensitive to accept these things."

"That's not being sensitive Laura. If it is then Gordon is too sensitive. We have talked about this between ourselves and Gordon is right to call it a great sin. That's exactly what it was. I was too much of a coward to own up to what I'd done. George Prentice never went to prison on account of anything I said, other folk did that to him. If I only had the guts to say it had been me, the poor man would have gone free but that's not how I felt at the time. Now somebody has done him in. It's a queer world, Laura. I don't blame you for being sensitive." Elda rambled. Her sentiments sounded tired and old and influenced by medication.

Laura turned to Gordon Macrae who was sitting quietly on the other side of the room.

"What are the doctors saying about Elda, Gordon?"

"Oh, they seem hopeful she can improve, Laura. They say it will take time and she will not be her normal self again but the outlook is not as bleak as we were first led to believe."

"That's good to hear, a bit of good news for a change." Laura Mackay said, turning her smiling face towards Elda.

"Thanks for phoning, Chief Inspector."

Fleming put the telephone down and considered the account Raymond Adam had just given him of the Aberdeen enquiry. He had told the Chief Inspector about the broken light lens in the grass at Lauradale and suggested that damage may have been the reason for the absence of the car during his visit to the PI premises. The man, Henry Dobson, sounded like the driver of the blue car but his description would fit so many others, including the stranger who had attended Prentice's funeral. This Colin Gibson did not sound like the type to go driving f or a hundred miles to break into a cottage during the day, but he was connected to Gregor Mackay by way of employment.

George Turnbull seemed ill-disposed towards George Prentice, a feeling retained from the time of his daughter's pregnancy and her secret letter to George in 1964. George Turnbull had been to Lauradale before, so would theoretically be able to return, but would he really go there in January to confront a much younger man? He did not sound like a physical match for the driver of the dark blue car. Most contrary of all considerations; he would not have been inclined to replace his daughter's letter.

The surprise visit to the Turnbulls in January from Gregor Mackay was interesting. Gregor Mackay had told Fleming that he had been in Florida at the time, a lie he had also told the Macraes. Lying about one's whereabouts at a material time is a red flag to a police officer. It generally means an attempt to create an alibi. So why did

Gregor Mackay feel the need to create an alibi in advance of George Prentice's murder?

The impression Raymond Adam had conveyed from the Turnbull's account of that unheralded home visit by Mackay seemed to reflect a rage by the American at a recent awareness, or suggestion, perhaps, that the man in his cottage was the biological father of his child. Taken in conjunction with the falsely created alibi that was unsupported by his wife and daughter, these circumstances gave Mackay the opportunity to carry out the murder of George Prentice. Did Mackay possess a key of his own for the cottage? Yes, he did. Fleming had asked the girl in the letting agency office. It was difficult now to see any stronger suspect than Gregor Mackay.

Raymond Adam had told Fleming that the lab had not yet reported back to him on the 1964 letter that Fleming had found at the cottage.

Fleming had discussed with Adam the need to let Mrs Rankine know that her brother was not now thought to be responsible for the rape and murder with which he had been charged. Adam agreed but would delay that message to Mrs Rankine until the legal process had dismissed her brother and decided on the action to be taken with Elda Macrae.

NINE

It was around two in the morning before Gregor Mackay reached Lauradale. Laura was asleep and he managed to get into bed without waking her.

Later that morning, a chirpy, smiling Laura brought her husband breakfast in bed, realising that he had been a late arrival the night before. Gregor Mackay mumbled his thanks but seemed begrudging of her favours. When he had risen and showered and dressed, he was more awake but still in a foul mood. He went to his office and unlocked the filing cabinet to remove the folder marked 'Arthur Fraser'. From a small cellophane bag within the folder he took the key for the cottage. Laura was watching him from the corner of the room.

"Right, he said. "We are going up to that cottage."

She realised that his mood was sour and angry. Not wishing to make matters worse, she merely lifted her quilted jacket from its peg and accompanied him. Unlike her stroll with Andrew Fleming this was more of a march towards an objective, the cottage of George Prentice. There was no conversation on the way. When they reached the cottage, Gregor unlocked the door and pushed it wide.

"Come in." he instructed. It was not an invitation, it was an order.

"I don't want to go in there." Laura protested.

"Why? Because he died in here? Well, I need you to be inside with me so come on." He sounded belligerent.

Laura had no idea what he had in mind or why he was so angry, but fearing his violence when no help was available, she went into the cottage lounge behind him. The place was cold and she shivered as she imagined George lying dead on the floor.

Gregor Mackay went over to the bookcase and began searching the titles on the right side of the shelves. Looking puzzled and frustrated, he looked along each shelf from right to left until he had seen every book. He had obviously failed to find what he had been looking for and his anger increased. He pulled all the books from the shelves until all books lay on the floor. This physical attack on the bookcase worried Laura and she had edged backwards towards the front door.

"Where are you going?" he roared at her. It was not really a question, more an instruction not to go any farther. She stopped.

Her husband went into the kitchen, then the bathroom and finally the bedroom. He emerged from the bedroom holding the empty photo frame.

"Did you remove this photograph?" he asked, making it sound like an accusation.

"I have never been in here." she protested. Her husband

seemed to think that this made sense and took the frame back to the bedroom.

"Right, let's go." he barked as he emerged from the bedroom. Whatever the point of this exercise had been it seemed to have failed and her husband was still angry and silent. As they walked back to the house Laura felt strangely vindicated and her husband's anger, while still smouldering, was now hopefully directed elsewhere.

When they reached the house Gregor Mackay told Laura, "I need to go back to Aberdeen." his voice was cold and uncaring.

"You do realise that we can count on one hand the number of days we have spent together here this year?" she said critically.

"Yea, well things could get worse." he warned. The telephone rang at that moment and he answered it. He seemed to listen carefully to what was being said but his expression remained sour. "Yeah. Okay, Colin, I'll just stay here."

As he replaced the phone he told Laura that he wouldn't be going to Aberdeen now. Things had changed.

"I'll be in the office." he said without enthusiasm.

That same morning Raymond Adam received a call from the CID in Aberdeen. The Grampian detectives had remembered that Adam had visited Aberdeen to carry out enquiry at the premises of A.P.I. Ltd with a particular car in mind.

"Did your interest include a man called Henry Dobson?" the Detective Inspector asked Adam.

"I think we can say that." Adam answered, "Although he threw us off track at the time. I would have wanted to speak to him again."

"I'm afraid that is not going to happen." the DI said apologetically. "He died in a road crash around two o'clock this morning on the M74 driving south about 12 miles north of Dumfries. He was alone in the car when he cut out to overtake a lorry in driving rain. The lorry driver said that was the first rain there had been on his journey. Dobson was driving 'way too fast' and just lost it, according to the lorry driver. The car went off the road before somersaulting. The lorry driver went to his aid but it was obvious to him that Dobson was dead. He called the police and ambulance. The Dumfries boys tell me that Dobson had ten thousand quid in cash on him."

"That's interesting. Can we have that cash retained for fingerprinting? What was the car he was driving?" Adam asked as various possibilities occurred to him simultaneously.

The DI gave him the registration number of a dark blue Ford, registered to A.P.I. Ltd.

"How do we know it is Dobson?" Adam asked.

"He had business cards for Henry Dobson of A.P.I. and he also fits the description. He never reported for work this morning. According to the receptionist, this man was a maniac driver, always speeding. He has nine points on his licence the Dumfries cop was telling me. The licence was in his wallet. Funny thing, apparently he also had a couple of business cards in his wallet for a 'Geoffrey Scott – HM Prisons Probation Services and a Glasgow number'." the DI told him.

That brought a dry laugh from Raymond Adam.

"Is the body in the morgue at Dumfries?" Adam asked expectantly.

"Yes. They want a post-mortem so I called Colin Gibson about that. Colin is an American oil company executive but he owns the P.I. firm and has met Dobson. He is happy to drive down for identification prior to post mortem. Dobson's ex-wife and family are in Newcastle. I called her and she will travel up tomorrow."

"I wanted a chance to meet this Colin Gibson, when is he going to be there?"

"Whenever he is wanted, he says. It looks like being tomorrow morning around ten. I have to call him back. He's a real gentleman, Colin Gibson. I think you'll like him."

"Tell him to look for me when he gets there. It'll save me another trip to Aberdeen. I am hoping to get Dobson's fingerprints when I go down tomorrow."

"I'll do that, Mr Adam."

Raymond Adam replaced the handset briefly before lifting it again. "Switchboard? Get me the CID at Dumfries will you?"

Douglas Campbell was invited to join the DCI the next

morning for the visit to Dumfries and he wasted no time in telling Andy Fleming.

"This man who has killed himself in a road accident is the same man who sent you and Adam to a wrong address, is that right?" Fleming asked seriously.

"Yes, Henry Dobson, a private investigator of some kind. Adam says he had ten grand on him when he died."

"Was that the firm's money?" Fleming suggested.

"No, at least nobody else is suggesting that. The DCI wants the money fingerprinted."

"I can see why." Fleming said with a nod of his head. "Anyway, have a nice day, as our American friends say."

Campbell went upstairs to inform MacKellar that he would be going to Dumfries in the morning. Fleming went through to negotiate a selling price with Charlie Macdonald for a twenty pack of Embassy tipped cigarettes. As they spoke the telephone rang and Charlie took it.

"It's for you, Andy. A Mr David Burnett, says he talked to you before."

"Hello Mr Burnett, what's new?" Fleming asked jovially.

"I have remembered what that rough character wanted to know about Laura Mackay's daughter. He asked me if the girl had dimples like her mother. It seemed a strange question to ask."

"Indeed, Mr Burnett. What did you tell him?"

"I told him that I really hadn't noticed if she had dimples or not but she was the spitting image of her mother. He seemed satisfied with that. I just thought I had better let you know before I forget all about it again."

"I am glad you did, Mr Burnett. It does help, so your call was worthwhile, thank you."

The following morning, shortly before ten o'clock, Raymond Adam and Douglas Campbell arrived at the mortuary of the Dumfries Hospital. In a corner of the car park a distressed woman in her late thirties was being comforted by a less distressed male of the same age. About twenty yards from them a well-dressed man of fifty or thereby stood talking to a pair of men in less expensive suits. Even from a distance Adam and Campbell could hear that the suave gentleman with shining silver hair was American. In this location it had to be Colin Gibson and sure enough, as distinctive as its owner, the new Mercedes stood out among the other vehicles in the car park.

The two CID officers who had been in conversation with Colin Gibson ensured that the persons present were introduced before entering the side door to the mortuary. There the covered body of Henry Dobson lay on a trolley in a small room with nothing to indicate the clinical purpose of the building. A middle aged man in hospital blues entered the room and smiled towards those present. He introduced himself as the pathologist and explained the nature and necessity of the procedure for identification of the deceased ahead of post-mortem examination. He was holding a clipboard and, as each person about to make identification was introduced by the local CID officer, the pathologist noted the name and relationship of the witness.

The former Mrs Dobson was invited to view the deceased first and managed the words, "Oh Harry." before turning away to be supported by her companion.

Colin Gibson waited for the lady to be ushered outside before he also stepped forward to look at the pale grey complexion of Henry Dobson.

"That is Henry Dobson." he said firmly, stepping back.

Raymond Adam was not really required to make identification but for future reference he wanted to be able to say that he had.

"That is the man who introduced himself to me as Henry Dobson three days ago." he stated with a nod to the pathologist.

The local CID officers showed Raymond Adam fingerprint forms they had prepared the previous day, duly completed with the prints of the deceased. He was given the option of taking his own if he preferred but he declined, a decision that seemed to please the pathologist.

"What about the possessions?" Adam asked. "The cash, the wallet and so on."

"It's all tagged and bagged, sir. We have them in a cardboard box in the car. There are also typed statements from us about our seizing them. Do you want to come back to the Police Office? It isn't far. If you and Mr Gibson just follow us in a moment there will be a room for you to speak to him in private."

"That sounds fine by me." the American said helpfully. Adam nodded.

"Just give me a second to say 'goodbye' to this lady and gentleman over there and I'll be right with you." the Dumfries detective asked politely.

As he parked at the Police Station, Raymond Adam could see the wreckage of a blue car sitting on an unmarked part of the yard.

"He broke more than a light lens this time." Adam muttered. "But that's the car we missed the other day, Dougie."

Douglas Campbell almost stepped into the path of Gibson's Mercedes as he gazed at the wreck and failed to hear the new car approach.

After a quick look at the possessions of the deceased Dobson and the CID statements referring to them, Adam signed for the items and took them with him as he joined Campbell and Gibson in a small interview room.

"I don't know how much you guys expect from me." Colin Gibson said with a smile. "I really never knew this man Dobson well, at all."

"To what extent did you know him?" Adam asked as he sat down.

"About three, maybe four, years ago our oil company was becoming a serious presence in Aberdeen. We knew by then that we would want and need a lot of local cooperation. Along with others we provided funding to help with non-oil related employment in the region. In this particular case, an entrepreneurial programme for locally based and staffed small businesses. There were several and just as varied as you might imagine. I was interested, I must admit, because I can appreciate the guts it takes to start up on your own nowadays. I was pretty busy myself but I did watch to see who was surviving and who was diving. I remember faces from the meetings with the local authority people and Dobson attended a couple of meetings that I was at but I never got to know him any better than anyone else."

"Surely this changed?" Adam said expectantly.

"Yes. It was maybe three years ago, or less, that my friend in the company, Gregor Mackay ... you know Gregor?"

"Yes we do." Adam confirmed.

"Well, Gregor and I go way back so he came to me and asked if I had any people who could track and stalk a man who was due to come out of prison and might pose a threat to the safety of his family. He never told me a name because he realised that I would not know the person and anyway, I was not getting involved. I suggested the police but he said, 'But the guy hasn't done anything yet'. I remembered that one of the start-up companies had been 'private-eyes' and I spoke to that Henry Dobson on the phone. Dobson said he could help as long as my friend had the money to pay him. He wanted my name and address as a sort of surety in case Gregor let him down. I gave him what he wanted 'cause I couldn't see that happening. I then put Gregor directly in touch with Dobson and I never heard another word about it. Occasionally I would ask Gregor how Dobson was doing and he would say that the man is still working on it."

"For three years?" Adam asked with incredulity.

Gibson laughed.

"Yeah. That's what I thought too. Apparently Dobson lost the scent for a while, something about the guy using another man's name, but you would have to speak to Gregor about that. He was not keen to keep me up to speed on this affair at all. I knew if he said things were going okay and smiled, things were okay. If he said things were fine 'but don't mention it' then things were not really going well. It was his private business but my only interest was that he and his family stayed safe. He never suggested to me that this was not the case, so I didn't pursue it."

"When we spoke to Dobson three days ago about that blue car he later crashed and died in, he said that you were the normal user of the car and you were carrying out work on your own behalf, using that blue Ford." Adam said seriously.

Colin Gibson looked at Adam as if he was mad.

"I have nothing to do with his blue Ford. I have just described to you what I know about the work being done and who his client actually was. I do not have time to carry on any work other than my own. You can see from my diary where I have been at any particular time in the past while, years even." Gibson complained.

"Fair enough, Mr Gibson." Adam said calmly. "Gregor Mackay was on holiday over Christmas and New Year, do you know when he started back?"

Gibson's brow furrowed as he thought about the question.

"He was off until the end of February, I think, or at least he was entitled to be off 'til then. He goes to Florida in the winter, has done for years."

"There was no work issue to bring him back sooner?"

"Not that I know of, Chief Inspector, and I would expect to know a thing like that." Gibson said in a relaxed way.

"The company has 'guest accommodation' in Aberdeen, is that so?" Adam said quietly.

"Yes, and Gregor uses it when he would have us all believe that he is too busy to go home." Gibson said with a smile.

"Is that often the case?" Adam asked easily.

"I would not have thought so, but Gregor works at his own pace and I have no reason to be near the guest accommodation personally. If I have friends over we all stay together at my house."

"You mentioned the private investigation business, this A.P.I. company that Dobson had, how well was it doing financially?" Adam asked seriously.

"I doubt that it was doing much at all." Gibson

replied. "Dobson would always tell you otherwise but he used to have three men beside himself. Now, he is alone with a part-time office girl. I did not hold out much hope for him."

"There were cars outside his office when we were there." Adam said quizzically.

"They probably belonged to the people next door, a courier firm. They are doing better, I believe. They start early and finish early every day. What you were seeing would have been employees' cars. Most of the firms in that industrial complex have had our assistance through the local authority scheme."

Adam and Campbell exchanged glances.

"Thanks for your time, Mr Gibson. You have been a great help to our understanding of this A.P.I. affair."

"You are quite welcome, Chief Inspector. Here is my card. Feel free to call me on anything else I might help you with."

Colin Gibson rose and, with a polite, 'Good day, gentlemen', left the room.

"I think we may have to go back to Aberdeen, sir." Campbell suggested.

"Not today." was the curt reply.

The pair had travelled twenty miles or more on their way home before either spoke.

"Did you get the impression that Gibson was suggesting that Mackay could be having an affair?" Campbell said.

231

"I did, Dougie. That could be one explanation for Dobson's ten thousand quid." Adam replied.

"Blackmail?"

"Of one kind or another, yes." Adam said with the air of someone whose meditation had been disturbed.

TEN

"You are off tomorrow, Andy, so you can take these two to the swimming pool."

David and Ann turned sharply to look at their father hopefully.

"Fair enough, we are going to the pool tomorrow." Andrew Fleming announced to the delight of his children. "We will go in the morning when it is a bit quieter, okay?"

"Yes and we can stay all day." his daughter suggested.

"You are only allowed to stay for an hour, remember?"

That afternoon Fleming was at work when Douglas Campbell returned from his visit to Dumfries. On the way back Campbell had failed to draw any thoughts from the mind of Raymond Adam, now he explained the events and conversations of the morning to Fleming in the hope of gaining some pointers. Better men than Campbell had attempted to extract thoughts and ideas from Fleming with the intention of forwarding them as their own.

"So there is a hint of blackmail in the air." Fleming said when the account had been completed. "But if the blackmail money was paid, why did Dobson still feel the need to run?"

"I think a lot of the answers lie in Aberdeen." Campbell suggested.

"I think you are right, Dougie. Is the big man planning on going back?"

"He is but he doesn't seem to be in any hurry." Campbell said disconsolately. "Anyway. It has been a long day. I'm off home."

Fleming watched him go. If Raymond Adam was in no hurry to follow a scent of blackmail in Aberdeen it would be based on assumption.

If there had been blackmail it would have occurred in Aberdeen, but probably based on events or facts at Lauradale. For Raymond Adam the known crime was still the local one, the murder of George Prentice. Any blackmail would only interest him if it helped him prove his murder case. If it simply concerned some ex-marital affair being conducted by Gregor Mackay in Aberdeen, how could that be relevant to the murder of George Prentice?

Contrary to Andrew Fleming's hopes and expectations the swimming pool was fairly busy the next morning. The school break was all too apparent in the numbers present. With his mind focussed on his own children, Fleming was surprised to hear a woman's voice in his ear.

"Are these lovely children yours, Mr Fleming?"

He turned to find Laura Mackay standing beside him in the shallow end of the pool.

"Yes they are, Mrs Mackay. They are and why I should be looking out for them, I don't know. They are better swimmers than I ever was. Is Mr Mackay with you? I thought he was down at the moment."

"No. He has gone back to Aberdeen, I'm afraid. He doesn't seem to be his usual self somehow." she said, as if resigned to a problem situation.

"What's wrong? Is it work?" Fleming asked innocently.

"No. I don't think it is work, not this time."

She went on to describe the visit she had made at her husband's insistence to Prentice's cottage. "I have no idea what he expected to find, Mr Fleming, but whatever it was, he never found it and he was mighty angry. Mind you, I had the feeling that he was ready to be just as angry if he had found whatever he was after."

Fleming realised that Gregor Mackay had been in search of the 1964 letter from his wife to Prentice but he said nothing to disclose his knowledge.

"Is there any possibility of your husband seeing someone in Aberdeen?"

"No, I don't really see him as that type. Why do you ask?" she said seriously.

"I am just considering the reasons, the normal or usual reasons if you like, for a man's disposition towards his wife to change." Fleming said, trying to sound nothing but rational. "If it isn't work and it isn't another woman,

235

could it be an undisclosed illness? Financial loss? Loss of status?"

Laura Mackay looked serious, a look that seemed unnatural for her.

"You are giving this more thought than I care to." she said.

"I'm sorry, I'm not helping because I do not really understand your husband's attitude, unless he has been aware of George Prentice all along."

"Who would have told him?" Laura Mackay objected.

"Your dad?" Fleming asked. The possibility had been on his mind for some time but he knew that the question, when put to Laura, could cause offence.

"Why would he do that?" Laura Mackay protested as if the suggestion was ludicrous. She turned and walked out of the pool. He should have known to expect this reaction. He had children to care for and he returned to them.

Gregor Mackay arrived at the premises of A.P.I. Ltd. in an angry mood. He found the place locked up with no sign of Henry Dobson. At the corner of the allocated parking area there was a portly girl with her head against the wall, weeping.

Mackay did not really feel inclined to speak to her but realised that things were out of the normal here. He went next door to the courier company and enquired.

"The place next door is locked up. I had hoped to meet

Henry Dobson there this morning. Has there been a development?" he asked.

"Mr Dobson died in a car crash the night before last." the receptionist told him apologetically. "It was on the radio this morning."

"Oh, I am sorry. I never heard. There is a girl outside crying ..."

"That's Jean, his receptionist. She hadn't heard either."

"Oh, I see, thank you."

News of Dobson's death shocked Mackay but his self-interest soon returned as he spoke to the distressed girl, Jean.

"I've only just heard about Henry Dobson." he said as sympathetically as he could. "Where did he have his accident?"

Jean looked at the cold, steely eyes of the American. She had seen him once before, in the office. He obviously did not remember her.

"Down near Dumfries." she said in a whimper.

"Isn't that near the border with England? Where was he going?" the question was cold and critical, almost insolent.

"I have no idea. It was two o'clock in the morning." she replied, her annoyance apparent.

Gregor Mackay simply turned and walked away in the direction of his car. Two o'clock in the morning two nights ago had been when he had arrived home to Lauderdale. Three hours earlier he had paid Dobson ten thousand pounds for information on where to find a letter his wife had written to George Prentice. The letter was supposed to be in the copy of 'Lorna Doone' on the bookshelf but there had been no such book. Mackay wanted his money back but how could he achieve that with Dobson now dead and the payment a matter of secrecy?

When she reached home from the pool, Laura Mackay telephoned her father.

"Dad, did you at any time tell Gregor about George Prentice being Lorna's father?" she said in voice that left her father in no doubt as to the importance of his answer.

He was quiet for a moment before he asked his own question. "He knows?"

"Yes dad, he knows, but certainly not from me."

"Laura, I don't remember everything I might have told him back when you and he first met because at times we were drinking together. When you two got engaged back in '65, he asked me about Lorna's natural father. He wasn't concerned about her being someone else's daughter, he already had accepted that, but he was afraid of some angry man turning up at his door someday. I told him that would not happen because the father was in prison and would be there for the next 17 years. He seemed to assume from what I said that you had been raped by this man and that Lorna was the result. It was natural that nobody wanted to talk about it. He never raised the subject with me again and he and I have never drunk together since."

"So, he did know." Laura said angrily.

"I never told him it was George Prentice." her father pleaded defensively.

"You told him enough for him to find out." she said in obvious rebuke.

"Is it going to cause a problem?" her father asked, sounding guilty.

"It already has." Laura said, still angry and for the first time in her life she put the phone down on her father.

When Fleming reached home with the children, Mary was ironing. After listening patiently to exaggerated accounts of swimming achievements, she told Andrew, "Raymond Adam phoned for you."

"He wants me to phone him?" Fleming asked, objecting to the idea of a lengthy and costly call to the DCI before midday.

Mary laughed. "I made the point myself." she laughed. "He is calling back at midday."

Fleming looked at the clock.

"There is not much we can do in twenty minutes, children. You can get your bikes out if you like."

On the stroke of noon, Raymond Adam called and apologised for the intrusion on Fleming's day off.

"I wanted to speak privately, Andy. Did Dougie Campbell tell you about Dumfries?"

"Yes he did." Fleming confirmed.

239

"What do you make of it, Andy? Is Mackay having an affair?"

Fleming laughed.

"I asked Mrs Mackay that very question this morning and she says 'no'."

Now Adam laughed.

"You asked her? What did you think she would say?"

"I met her at the swimming pool. She and her husband are not on the best of terms at the moment and she was wondering what might be eating him. He has gone back to Aberdeen. There is more though." Fleming then recounted Laura Mackay's account of the enforced visit to the cottage to search for a book he never found and his subsequent rage at not finding it."

"He expected to find the letter inside the 'Lorna Doone' book and confront his wife with it." Adam deduced. "Had he been the one to place the book there, do you suppose?"

"No, I don't think so and for the same reasons I do not think he killed George Prentice either."

"All right, Sherlock, how do we prove any of this?" Adam said sarcastically.

"Dougie Campbell took fingerprints from Gregor Mackay when his picture was reported stolen. Do we still have these?" Fleming asked hopefully.

"No, they will be destroyed by now, they were only for elimination prints in a case that died of natural causes. They could not be used for comparison with anything on the poker. That was what you had in mind?"

"We can still get Mackay's prints if we get back into that cottage. Fleming suggested. "According to his wife he was the last person to handle the photograph frame in the bedroom. It was clean prior to that."

"How do you know that?" Adam asked sceptically.

"Because the second last person wiped it clean" Fleming said confidently.

"Oh, then that second last person would know." Adam said with mock annoyance.

"Wouldn't it be easier and a bit more legal just to speak to Gregor Mackay about the mass of circumstantial stuff against him and take his fingerprints then?"

"Sure," Fleming agreed. "When will that be?"

"I have been waiting for urgent comparison of prints taken from Dobson and the poker, the bookcase and the letter. I got the results this morning. Now I am awaiting the comparison results of the prints we get from the cash that Dobson was carrying."

"That could be where Gregor Mackay steps back into the picture." Fleming commented.

"So, assuming that the prints of Mackay and Dobson are both on the cash, what are you making of this?" Adam invited Fleming to speculate.

"I think that Mackay was employing Dobson to track down George Prentice. Exactly what the instructions were I don't know but I believe Dobson killed Prentice and pulled the bookcase down on top of him. It may have been then that the letter fell from the 'Lorna Doone' book.

Dobson read the letter before placing it in one of Prentice's food containers and burying it in the garden. He held Mackay to ransom over the letter, preventing Mackay from saying anything about the murder. When the death was reported the garden looked quite normal and then later it was covered by snow that melted. When he thought it safe to do so, Dobson returned to dig up the letter and return it to the 'Lorna Doone' book. He had to dig a bit more because he could not readily identify the exact spot where it was buried. I am guessing that Mackay then had to pay Dobson ten thousand pounds for information leading to the letter. I dare say that Dobson would testify, if ever questioned, that he simply identified George Prentice to Gregor Mackay and the murder must then be down to Mackay. Why would Dobson kill him?"

"Why would he?" Adam asked.

"Because Prentice disturbed him at the cottage?" Fleming suggested.

"You could be right." Adam said in a congratulatory tone. "The fingerprint evidence will support our line of questioning by supporting or destroying your version. When I have that evidence we can speak to Gregor Mackay again."

"Am I being invited this time?" Fleming asked cheekily. "We will wait and see about that." Adam said with a broad smile that Fleming was unaware of.

"Yes, Mrs Macrae, there is a slight improvement in

your blood but I see no increase in your weight." the physician said as he looked into Elda's eyes from the other side of the table. "You must find more appetite from somewhere. We cannot force feed you."

"I can't eat any more, doctor, I would make myself sick." Elda protested.

"You will not be sick if you eat little and often, Mrs Macrae, not too much at a time. You understand what I am getting at Mr Macrae?"

Gordon nodded his head but said nothing. The doctor had not witnessed Gordon's struggle to encourage Elda to eat anything at all.

"Get yourself out in the fresh air if you can. Walk as much as you are able. It is vital that you encourage your body to do what it can for itself. I cannot increase your medication but you may be able to increase its effectiveness." the doctor urged. "Without that effort on your part you may lose the battle."

He smiled at her but Elda's face was devoid of expression or hope.

"Do what you can and I hope to see you back here in two weeks. By then we will have today's blood test results." he said pleasantly.

"Hello, Mr Gibson? It's Raymond Adam here. Just let me know if I am interrupting you there."

"Not at all, Chief Inspector, how are you? I'm just going over some graph scales, what can I do for you?"

"You and Gregor Mackay go back to your college days, is that right?" Adam asked tentatively.

"We sure do. What's on your mind?"

"I am going into discussions shortly with the Mackays and the enquiry line doesn't bother me but I want to avoid eggshells if I can. I understand that Gregor was married before and then divorced back in the U.S. Can you tell, just between you and me, what lay behind that divorce?"

Colin Gibson lowered his voice to answer.

"Jealousy. Gregor accused his wife of affairs and Lord knows all what. The poor girl could scarcely afford to say 'hello' to any man under eighty without him accusing her. I have been his friend for a long time, Chief Inspector, but believe me. I would avoid his wife when he wasn't with her. They broke up on account of his unfounded suspicions but she claimed mental cruelty. She was right and he was wrong but you can't change that in a man like Gregor. I always saw his move to a quiet country place as his way of addressing the same issues where Laura was concerned. Like his first wife, Laura is attractive and he instinctively expects her to be attracted to other men and other men to her. It's simply paranoia."

"Is he a man to have affairs himself?" Adam asked.

"No sir, he's not and he is never off my radar. He couldn't step out of line without my knowing or suspecting it. I don't miss much."

"I am obliged to you Mr Gibson. This conversation will not be repeated or referred to but it will help. Thank you."

When he had finished with Gibson, Raymond Adam lifted the phone again to call the CID in Aberdeen. He asked for a statement to be obtained from the receptionist at A.P.I. Ltd and faxed to him by the next morning. He then explained exactly which questions he particularly wanted to be answered.

At two o'clock the following afternoon, Fleming joined Raymond Adam and Douglas Campbell at Lauradale. Gregor Mackay was at home and had no solicitor with him. His wife did not stay after the police arrived but excused herself to go and visit the Macraes.

Her leaving allowed the police officers to move about the lounge and ensure that she had left no recording devices behind. Fleming had warned that she might do so but there were none to be seen on this occasion.

When all four men were seated, Raymond Adam looked intently at Gregor Mackay as he explained to him the reason for their visit. Mackay actually appeared nervous.

"Right Mr Mackay, why did you pay Henry Dobson the sum of ten thousand pounds in cash on the night of Tuesday 13th. of March?"

Mackay hesitated before replying.

"Because I had employed him and I was due him the money." he said warily.

"For what specific purpose had you employed Henry Dobson?"

"He is a private investigator. I first employed him about three years ago to find the identity of a man who had committed a rape back in 1963 and been sentenced to eighteen years in prison as a result."

"Why did you want such a man traced?" Adam asked in the same quiet tone. He could see that Mackay was trying to buy himself time to think.

"I wanted to ensure that he stayed away from my family once he was released." Mackay said defensively.

"Why did you think that his release could bring any attention from him on your family?"

"He had once been attracted to Laura, my wife, and he might well try to track her down." his voice reflected some of the anxiety that Gibson had spoken of.

"Would he have any particular reason to be 'hunting down' your wife, as you put it?" Adam pressed.

"He was my daughter's natural father." he said quietly, as if ashamed by his answer. He stared down at his carpet. He had not enjoyed making the statement.

"Did you know the name of this man?"

"Not at first. That was part of Dobson's remit. He went around press libraries and came up with the name 'George Prentice'. With Prentice due for release from prison I asked Dobson to keep surveillance on this Prentice to see if he was making any move to follow Laura or Lorna."

"And did he?" Adam asked, feeling impatient at the slowness of the conversation.

"Dobson lost the trail for a while and when he caught up with Prentice he found that he was staying at Lauradale under the name Arthur Fraser. The bloody man had been right under my nose on my own property for two years. Dobson asked me what I wanted done with Prentice. I told him that I was going to Florida with my family until the start of the year. He could use the time to devise ways to discourage Prentice to leave Lauradale. Of course, at that time I only had Dobson's word that this was George Prentice." Mackay said shamefully. "I still wanted the man gone."

"Did that include killing him?" Adam asked.

"No, not at all, that was never even suggested as a joke. Dobson had said nothing to suggest doing such a thing and neither did I. I came back earlier than planned because I had called Dobson from Florida for a progress report and found that he had been sitting on his hands while accepting my regular expenses payments. I was angry. I told Dobson to act immediately or my money to him would stop."

"What was he supposed to do?" Adam asked in the same even tone as before.

"He had been given three months to figure that out but had wasted his time. I told him, man to man, to get positive on this. What he later told me was that he had gone to Prentice, masquerading as a probation officer. He had told Prentice to report to Barlinnie Prison within the week for a discipline hearing. If he failed to turn up then a warrant would be issued for his arrest."

"So, what happened?" Adam asked.

"Prentice didn't buy it, apparently. He said he was quite happy being where he was and who he was. Dobson could please himself but he wasn't moving. I think Dobson just lost it at that point and hit him with something." Mackay sighed. "He hadn't expected to kill the man but he knew that he had done, so he pulled the bookcase down on top of Prentice in the hope of making it look like an accident. I told him that he hadn't fooled anyone, the police were treating it as murder. He told me to give him ten thousand pounds and he would disappear somewhere where he could not be found. If I refused to pay him as I suggested I would, he would inform the police that I had killed Prentice out of rage and jealousy, something I am unfortunately known for. If the police needed evidence then he would lead them to a letter my wife had written to Prentice in prison. He knew where the letter was because he had found it in Prentice's pockets after the man was dead. If I paid him he would tell me where to find the letter myself."

Mackay was not enjoying this account of his but was speaking nervously and quickly in a manner suggesting admission rather than invention.

"So you decided to pay him?" Adam said.

"Only when he had told me where to find the letter." Mackay said. "He told me but he was lying, the book wasn't there."

Adam glanced at Fleming before resuming.

"Did it never occur to you to simply open up the truth

of the situation at Lauradale with everyone knowing who everyone else was?" Adam suggested.

Mackay looked at Raymond Adam as if his suggestion was ridiculous.

"My daughter Lorna in the same place as her natural father? My wife in the same place as the man who had raped her? Do you think I wanted that?" Mackay protested.

"Mr Mackay, the man served eighteen years in prison but you are the only one in this room who still believes that George Prentice ever raped or killed anyone. The man served time for raping and killing Elda Macrae's daughter and even Mrs Macrae knows that he didn't do that." Adam said plainly. He sat back but continued to look directly at Gregor Mackay.

"Mr Mackay, I want you to look at this from a different standpoint, beginning with the personal reasons you have just given for wanting rid of George Prentice. Add to that the deceit of your coming home from Florida one week into January despite telling your neighbours, and afterwards the police, that you came home on Sunday the 27th of January. This puts you here in Scotland when George Prentice was killed with you lying, after the event, about where you had been at the time. You had the same opportunity to commit this murder as Henry Dobson. Dobson knew all along that you wanted rid of Prentice and when he learns that Prentice is dead he sees a chance to blackmail you. Do you in your innocence report him to the police for blackmailing you? No. You pay the man ten thousand pounds. He believes then that you certainly did want him to kill Prentice so he does not hang around for one moment longer and speeds south, bringing about his own death in the process." Adam paused and spread his hands apart.

"Which version am I to believe?"

Gregor Mackay looked stunned and lent forward, clasping his hands and looking aimlessly at the carpet.

"I have been very stupid. I can see that now." Mackay said meekly. "After I paid him the cash he told me that he could afford to accuse me of conspiracy if the police caught up with him, so I had better keep my mouth shut. If I chose otherwise he would tell the police that I had paid him to kill George Prentice. I had been too naïve to see that coming. If Dobson was alive today, he would have me in knots."

"But he is dead now and by his own hand. Thankfully for you there is a witness to Dobson's death." Adam said in a matter of fact manner.

Mackay uttered a sarcastic 'Huh', then said quietly, "I could never have killed him anyway." he spoke as if admitting to a disappointing failure in his character.

"You are left-handed are you not?" Adam asked.

"Yes, I am." Mackay said, looking up in surprise. "Does that make me guilty of something?"

Raymond Adam laughed.

"Only of being left-handed, Mr Mackay. I think we

have heard all that we need." Turning to Campbell and Fleming, he asked, "You chaps got any questions for Mr Mackay?"

Fleming looked directly at Gregor Mackay and asked, "When was the last time you hit someone, Mr Mackay?"

Gregor Mackay was taken aback by the question and he seemed stuck for an answer. "I … I don't know. I don't remember ever hitting anyone." he said a little ashamedly.

"Fair enough." Fleming replied. "But you did tell Dobson to attend George Prentice's funeral in order to know whether Mrs Mackay attended or not?"

"Yes, part of my jealous self, I'm afraid."

"That's good to hear." Adam said as he stood up and offered Mackay an outstretched hand. "Thank you for your time, Mr Mackay. I will be reporting all the circumstances to the Procurator Fiscal and he will make the decisions on any further proceedings. I don't expect you will receive any worrying correspondence."

As the police officers were walking back to their cars Fleming heard Raymond Adam mumble something about 'another of your bloody stunts'. Fleming just laughed. These grumpy old guys could be so amusing.

"Why do you believe him?" Dougie Campbell asked Raymond Adam, nodding back in the direction of the Mackay house.

"I got a faxed statement down from Aberdeen this morning, Dougie. They had spoken to Jean Simons, Dobson's receptionist, the girl we saw in his office. She told the CID that the firm was basically broke and Dobson was desperate. The day we were in his office he had admitted to her that he had made one hell of a mistake and as soon as his car was fixed he was getting 'to hell out of there'. He shut the office early that day just as we thought. When he got his car back he was going to 'screw more money out of him' but he told Simons that it wouldn't be enough to save the company from going under. He had promised to send money to her and he left her the keys of the office. At no time did he ever say that Mackay was guilty of anything. She was specifically asked that question and whether Dobson was right-handed. He was."

"So Dobson killed Prentice." Campbell said with a nod of his head.

"His fingerprints were on the handle of the poker, upwards and anti-clockwise, the grip of a right-handed man." Adam said. "The same prints were on the bookcase, the lid of the food container, the book of 'Lorna Doone' and the 1964 letter from Laura Turnbull to George Prentice."

He turned to Fleming.

"I told you that fingerprints would make or break your reasoning, Andy."

"Oh yes, you are right about fingerprints, sir, but they are no substitute for a street education."

Raymond Adams laughed and shook his head.

Fleming sat in a room of the office looking at the list of

items he had to catch up on. None of it was the least bit interesting. The phone rang and he took the call.

"Constable Fleming, it is Margaret Rankine. I am just calling to thank you for the notepad, it arrived this morning. George never wrote very much just as you say, but I take comfort from the thought that he wanted to write to me at all. I was so wrong about him."

"Yes, I imagine he was literally lost for words, Mrs Rankine. He would have hoped to convince you that he was innocent." Fleming said sympathetically.

"I have had a visit from young Lorna Mackay, you know. She seems to have heard from other people that George had not committed these crimes at all. Is there any truth in that?"

Fleming found the question awkward.

"I am not really empowered to tell you the truth of the suggestion, Mrs Rankine, simply because of my employment. I am sure you will be informed in some official way in due course. In the meantime, enjoy what Lorna has to say. She is a lovely girl and easy to like. What made her travel down to see you?"

"I had invited her when I met her at George's funeral. I told her that she and I should get together sometime. She has helped me with things that matter to me."

"What kind of things, Mrs Rankin? I would be happy to help you in any way I can."

"Oh, we just spoke about family life when George and I were young. She has helped me to choose a headstone for

George and so on, just the comforting things that two women can provide for each other, Mr Fleming. You have already helped in a practical way, Mr Fleming and made the truth appear at last. I am most grateful."

"It has been a pleasure to put matters right, especially in your mind, Mrs Rankine. Thank you for calling."

This call from Mrs Rankine reminded Fleming of a call he ought to have made by now. He looked in his notebook for the number.

"Alison, it is Andrew Fleming. How are things with your mum?"

"She is doing well thank you, Mr Fleming. We expect her home by next Monday. If that goes well, I hope to be on a plane home by the middle of the week. I am missing my little Emma and she is missing her mom."

"That all sounds very satisfactory, Alison. I wish you all well. You have been an enormous help in setting the record straight."

In his notebook Fleming had noticed the name and telephone number of Jock Cameron.

With less enthusiasm but a sense of propriety, Fleming called the old detective to explain how his case of twenty-two years earlier had been ripped apart by the new evidence of Alison Swarbeck and Elda Macrae. It was not an easy conversation and Jock Cameron realised that. He thanked Fleming for calling him personally to explain the outcome of his investigation.

Three weeks later, Elda Macrae passed away in her sleep. Gregor and Laura Mackay gave Gordon Macrae assistance with the funeral arrangements. Gordon never received an invoice from anyone. Fleming was among the mourners and was pleased to see that Jimmy Johnston had brought Jock Cameron to the funeral.

After the graveside part of the funeral service was over, Andy Fleming invited J.J. and Jock to see where George Prentice was buried. All three were slightly surprised to see a newly erected stone in grey marble that read, 'In Loving Memory of GEORGE PRENTICE – Born 1940 – Died 1985 – A much loved father brother and friend'.

"A father?" Jock asked. "When was he a father?"

"When you locked him up." said Fleming. "His daughter and her mother were both at his funeral."

Jock Cameron looked at Fleming with a puzzled frown.

"What was the mother's name?"

Jimmy Johnston chuckled.

"Her name was Laura. She was Laura Turnbull, the Laura he couldn't hurt. She is Laura Mackay nowadays." Fleming answered the question, nodding at the headstone. "He would never admit to being unfaithful to Laura Turnbull then, she would have been hurt by it, but they are friends again now."

The author is retired but his professional life was spent in law enforcement. An operational career in Scottish police forces was followed by roles in private health security, aviation security, civil law process and Scots Law proofing.

He is a husband, father and grandfather and now resides in Edinburgh.

GEORGE MURRAY BOOKS

Justice for Jenny and Judas

Evil Issue

Blind Love Blind Hate

The Fleming Series

The Weed Killer

Mrs Livingstone's Legacy

A Tale of Old Comrades

The Tale of the Old School Ties

Fur and Feathers

Lightning Source UK Ltd.
Milton Keynes UK
UKOW02f2153020816

279809UK00001B/1/P

9 780992 738587